HAPPY

HALLOWEEN

SCARY BASTARD

ARON BEAUREGARD

ISBN: 9781073070947

Cover & Interior Art Copyright © 2020
Anton Rosovsky

Original Bonus Art Copyright © 2019
Andriy Dankovych

Halloween Night Art Copyright © 2019
Katherine Burns

Cover Wrap Design Copyright © 2020
Don Noble

Edited by Laura Wilkinson

Printed in the USA

Maggot Press
Coventry, Rhode Island

<u>WARNING</u>
This book contains scenes and subject matter
that are disgusting and disturbing, easily
offended people are not the intended audience.

JOIN MY MAGGOT MAILING LIST NOW
FOR EXCLUSIVE OFFERS AND UPDATES
BY EMAILING
AronBeauregardHorror@gmail.com

WWW.EVILEXAMINED.COM

For Jose Acevedo who always supported my work and ideas no matter how extreme or unconventional.

You will forever be missed but your memory lives on.

THIS HALLOWEEN THE SANITARIUM DOORS HAVE OPENED
FOR SPINE-TINGLING SAMHAIN SLAUGHTER!

SCARY BASTARD

ARON BEAUREGARD

"Bad times don't last, but BAD GUYS do."

- Scott Hall

MALL RAT

The twins were like a BOGO deal. Hershel had only forecasted a single kidnapping, but magically, there happened to be two. He couldn't have felt more blessed. Almost every guardian has let their kids take a run through the mall for a few hours when they were growing up. Hanging out, getting into trouble, and window-shopping was like a rite of passage for the young.

Mom pulled up and handed the 15-year-olds a twenty spot each, then let the identical teens run loose. They were ready to rifle through all of the pointless products that the building offered, while mom and dad went down the road a few blocks for Mai Tai's and a basket of crab rangoons. While they were sharing the leftover cheese and imitation crab meat, their girls would be dreaming about purchasing a few high-ticket items and chattering about the cute boys at school.

Being around teenagers could make you crazy, Hershel knew the spot all too well. The struggle of being a parent, raising good, honest kids in a world contaminated by immorality. It was a lot of pressure, so when your kids are rational enough to be on their own for a few hours and afford you a breather (no matter how pathetic the pardon), it's rousing. He could see the revival openly in their body language, they were set for, at minimum, an hour of indulgence.

So many reasons these young ones make me wanna pull all my hair out—too many to count. Look at 'em, oh to be young again. When you're fledgling, you think you already know everything, but once you get gray, you realize you never knew shit. They don't see it yet but they sure as hell will. Everybody does. Everybody that has the privilege of growing old that is… Eventually, we all just revert back to being babies again, doleful, floundering elders. While our cognizance has become comprehensive and our minds that hold encyclopedic knowledge are so much wiser, they've also deteriorated. Literally rotted away. Until we wake up one day and find ourselves dependent on the next wave we've created. It's a vicious cycle, one that leaves a parent crossing their fingers, hoping that they did a good enough job. We should be scared. Our survival, in many ways, will be contingent upon it, Hershel thought.

Hershel had come to understand that knowledge obtained isn't always such a routine practice to disperse back, especially into the next generation. Sometimes people don't want to hear words besides their own. They just want to stick their fingers in the light-socket a few times and learn for themselves. The immature filtered only the trivial percentage of what the patriarch preached, the smaller fractions that conveniently aligned with their own unseasoned beliefs. To them, life—and those who knew what it was to be beaten down by it—could offer no lessons.

It drove Hershel crazy at the time, but he found a way to stick it out. Working at a sanitarium and being a single father to three young girls was a real satirical dynamic. At work, he was the orderly; at home, he was closer to the patient. He didn't have to work there. Based on the cash he'd accumulated from Madeline's passing, he didn't have to work at all. But the part of him that remained unexposed (publicly anyway) enjoyed it.

Seeing the caged freaks, the absurdity of their discussions and the pathetic nature of their days was elevating to his persona. It was a self-harvested shot in the arm, an intoxication that served to help him understand that his own sickness could be so much worse. Instead of feeling like the piece of shit he was, it shaped the illusion not that he was mentally healthy, but at least healthier.

He might have issues but at least he could hide them. The people locked away in there just let it all hang out. It was the only thing that gave him confidence that the glue would hold… that he wasn't falling apart. Frankly, it was the only thing that kept him sane.

His girls were grown now, but he could remember on so many occasions wanting to kill them—both figuratively and literally. He couldn't though for a few different reasons. First of all, they were his kids, no matter how much he'd come to regret them. Secondly, there was a lesser part of him that wanted to see them succeed, if not for themselves then so they could tend to him once he'd finally lost his marbles. No matter how much of an annoyance and hindrance on his life they'd been, no matter the unspeakable lust teasing his brain with the idea nibbling at his ear, killing them just wasn't feasible.

Maybe things wouldn't have felt like they did if his wife, Madeline, hadn't been T-boned by a semi-truck. Maybe he wouldn't be alone staring coldly at these innocent young girls as they wondered carelessly with no idea of the sinister scheme hatching around them. Still, even if he wasn't stalking them, he would certainly be dreaming about it. Salivating a warm clear reservoir at the thought of his potential wickedness.

The fleeting memories of Madeline brought to mind the burden he'd been assigned—identifying her body, or what remained of it. It was like trying to put a puzzle together, except you couldn't move any of the pieces. Sure, it was her theoretically… the chunks were scooped out of her demolished Jeep Cherokee, which bore her license plate and was found on the route she took home from the office. It was difficult to confirm since she'd become a cyclone of flesh, but as unbelievable as the outcome was, it had to be her. Madeline was dead.

One drowsy driver falling asleep at the wheel can have an incredible impact on the future. The girls went to their mother's closed casket before two of them had even gone to their first day of school. He noticed how the early life tragedy shifted their young souls, filling them with resentment and animosity. It fell on him to explain how life was still fair, even though they hardly knew their mother before she became a cluster of munchies for the maggots. It was his responsibility to lie to them.

He couldn't help but wonder if things would have been different if Madeline was still alive. It could have been them sneaking away for a drink at the Chinese restaurant. It could have been his girls thankfully skipping through the mall. His mind could have been occupied by the nectarous devotion they had for each other, rather than being left to its own devices. It seemed that destiny just didn't have that in the cards though.

Boredom is evil's most refined yet unnoticed tool. It seems harmless in theory, but when given some room, if the puppy is sick enough, the output can be bone-chilling. It lets one's internal contemplations tour places they might not ordinarily. For Hershel, it created a portal to perversion. A sanctuary for sin. It brought him to a dark place that was only paralleled by the deplorable inmates confined to the cold cells of the Ladd Institute where he worked.

It was all so captivating and powerful. The fact that he was able to keep a lid on it while still living with his children was a testament to his self-restraint. It showed that he wouldn't just be some one-and-done idiot who shot up the cafeteria or brought a bomb to the bus station. He knew once the day of reckoning was initiated, he'd have a long, successful run.

Irrespective to the history of unfair and wicked events triggered by his wife's tragic demise, Hershel had managed to control himself, to control his hunger. He served as a protector and gave the bratty threesome he'd spawned a pretty damn good life in his eyes. His mind was largely elsewhere during the upbringing, but thinking about the horrors he might accomplish once his kids matured and moved on didn't stop him from giving them an admirable childhood.

To him, you didn't have to be a good person to be a good father. The two concepts weren't married to each other. As long as he was killing *other people's* kids, he could still be a hero to his own. Considering he was a single dad for the entire run, he looked at three high school diplomas and a college enrollment as a major underdog victory.

He was still robbed of any semblance of a personal life for the majority of their maturation, "crab rangoon-less" so to speak. He spent the timeline doing two things primarily: making sure the girls had all they needed for success or dealing with the loonies' violent outbursts and ramblings of madness. Over time, it was that combination that seemed to turn the atmosphere terminal.

He was now only interested in freeing people from the shackles of their parental existence. Or maybe that was just something he told himself to justify the stroking of his own perverse sex drive. He was trying to convince himself that he was killing two birds with one stone, but in reality, he was just smashing one to a gory pulp.

He liked them young for the unarguable fact that they were a lot more naïve and easier to acquire than young adults. Deep down, whether they were in middle school or high school made no difference to him. He was equally enticed by anyone in the range that fell under the legal drinking age. Everything after that seemed to contradict the true spirit of what he was allegedly trying to accomplish—freedom for the parents at the price of obscene gratification for himself.

He'd developed some intriguing tactics that he drew directly from his own experiences being a dad. His past had granted him a more attuned command on how to manipulate his victims and lay out a blueprint. He was ready to showcase the refinements he'd made over his dozen or so previous victims. He'd become a well-oiled murder machine, with an intellectually thoughtful process. Meticulous attention to every facet of his crimes would ensure the marathon of manslaughter he was positioning himself for would go uninterrupted.

The twins' mommy and daddy were just about to be heading down the road for a few minutes and get themselves a small break from the daunting cycle of parenting. Little did they know, Hershel was about to make it a permanent one.

You're welcome, he thought to himself, watching the Chevy minivan pull away. The girls raced through the rotating glass doors of the mall, no doubt pondering how they would spend their twenty big ones. It was easy to tell the girls were doppelgangers by their faces and hair, but they each dressed totally contrary to the other.

One had baggier black pants and a Coal Chamber t-shirt. She no doubt was the "artist" of the pair. The goth's parents had allowed her to flood her eye rims with a thick black liner and even shade her lips with a cloudy black licorice tone (which, by Hershel's parenting standards, she seemed a bit young for). Her fists had almost as many silver rings as she had fingers. Multiple necklaces with strange symbols hung around her neck, causing her to appear to either be a believer of numerous religions or maybe none at all. Her parents hadn't let her dye her hair yet but you could tell she was desperate to. He guessed that the eccentric girl would not be allocating funds toward eating, instead she'd be spending her twenty at Hot Topic.

The other sister was bright colored and basic—no graphic designs on her clothing and no jewelry of any sort. Neither of them looked really girly, so he assumed she was probably some kind of athlete. Her shoe selection was not aimed toward being a fashion statement so much as it was to get the best relay-race time. Her skin was also a shade or two more tan than her sister. She was probably involved in some youth recreational sport was Hershel's guess. He was betting that she'd be looking at Footlocker or Olympia Sports with her leisure allowance. He also saw a fruit shake of some sort in her near future, Orange Julius was seeming highly probable.

Their walk and mannerisms were very similar, and judging from their interaction, they weren't just siblings but also the best of friends. Despite the fact that they were a contradictory couple—polar opposites that were still somehow the same—it was a prime example of the old opposites attract law, except they had identical DNA anyway so it seemed more logical. He'd never really interacted with twins in person before but he'd seen many shows that detailed their deep internal and occasionally supernatural bond. It sure was going to be interesting if he could get a chance to talk to them.

Hershel had been inside dozens of malls but never the same one a third time. His first visit was reserved for an attention to detail casing. He'd usually spend the entirety of one full day, from almost open to close, lingering around inside the mall. Inspecting all exits and entryways—the lesser used, the better. Restrooms were also a big point of research. They were a place where he could potentially find his prey alone and more vulnerable. Parking garages and security camera locations also needed to be noted, which he did, down to the most insignificant particulars.

Loading areas were of specific interest to him as he usually dedicated a few more weeks of his time to understanding the delivery patterns and exterior infrastructure of the building. He didn't want to miss any windows of opportunity that might present themselves, wherever they might be hiding.

After his period of targeted snooping was a wrap, he separated himself from the mall, usually for at least a month. Just long enough so that the film of his prior visit would be forgotten, but not too long to where the details weren't still relatively fresh in his mind. Long enough so he was able to weave a mental spider web within every inch of the wonderful walls of retail, and long enough that the consumers were entangled without even realizing it… until the predator was a blink from plunging his fangs deep inside of them.

That day had finally come, and thus, so had Hershel. He'd never taken two at once but his ego was egging him on. It was enticing him and drilling thoughts through his mind. Luring him closer to complete seduction with the potential that an event like the one he'd been preparing for could have.

A sick man like himself only lived for these times. Only the commission of the most extreme atrocities would allow him to achieve his baleful zenith. Today would be the day that the rest of his life began. He had a familiar yet unique feeling circulating within his skull and veins.

The Emerald Square Mall, surprisingly, had a very limited number of cameras on the first three floors of the main track. These were just walking areas primarily, theft and crime were typically set to occur inside the stores, each of which was fitted with multiple recording devices. One point of exception was the food court on the third floor… that was a hot zone in his estimation. Unlike the remainder of the primary corridor, that area was littered with recorders. He'd be staying clear of it without exception.

Hershel was dressed plainly, wearing dull colors, the farthest thing from flashy. Not that he was some snazzy dresser anyway, but this was plain Jane even for him. Deceptively lightweight running shoes that looked appropriate for almost any occasion, flexible tan pants, and a zip-up navy-blue hoodie were his outfit of choice. He was also wearing a baseball cap that had a statue of liberty embroidery in the center of it. People liked and trusted patriotism but it was so common that it often went unnoticed.

The fitted ball cap was discretely wired with an LED bulb, which, on command, he could remotely activate. If he got in a pinch, he could use it to obscure his face momentarily from the surveillance cameras. The light would not be highly visible to other patrons but if they did happen to see it, he hoped they'd think it was just a cool design.

The benefits it provided him were twofold. If the bill of the hat was angled appropriately, it helped obscure his face from others, and when the light was activated, surveillance recordings would not pick up his face. Instead, they would capture his entire head as a streaky distorted white orb. It was a nifty invention that anyone who's burgled a surveyed location would know about. He'd set himself up to avoid detection and make a clean sweep.

Hershel was holding a black shopping bag with an EbLens logo on the side of it. Inside, he carried his tools of deception and his fingertips were becoming more eager with each stride he took. The girls had strolled about the second floor, hovering a bit while they chatted.

The middle floor would have been his preference since it usually had the least amount of traffic. He trailed the twins loosely, never giving them an inkling that they were being watched or followed. They'd passed a hollow Spirit of Halloween store that management was still yet to fill up the shelves of completely. They'd better hurry, Hershel's favorite holiday wasn't too far away.

He loved Halloween because it was the one night when you could be yourself and no one would be the wiser. He could show his true colors and everyone just took it in jest since it was meshed into an array of silliness that was the globe's most intriguing dress-up day. There were so many kids out and about on Devil's Night and he wanted to send all of them to the abyss. He'd fleshed out some of his creativity previously on Halloween but still felt like his definitive masterpiece was yet to be conjured. He knew there would be new opportunities in the future, he could feel it. He just didn't know what they were yet...

He could think about the prospect all day but the twins were slowing down near the Orange Julius stand as he suspected they might. He only had a few minutes to think about the next move and didn't waste time patting himself on the back in light of his accurately forecasted foreshadowing. Instead, he ventured toward the fire alarm hanging from the wall by the JC Penney.

Hershel retrieved a small red metallic contraption he had manufactured from his EbLens bag. He looked around to make sure he wasn't being watched before slipping it into the trigger slot. It sat snugly, filling the same space one's hand would when pulling to activate the alarm. It was rooted electronically to the same remote that his hat was and would perform a different but similarly valuable task if things fell into place like he was expecting.

He drifted off into the backdrop just as before, lurking and stalking the girls carefully. Their next movements made his heart race, it must have been a long drive because they were headed for the bathroom. This particular lavatory was seldom used, being on the most unpopular of all the floors, which was known for children's clothing stores and nauseatingly scented candles. Beside the restrooms, he'd noted that there was an emergency exit that led out into the parking garage, which was conveniently not too far from where his vehicle sat waiting. Now all that was left for him to do was create an emergency.

Once the girls had disappeared down the end of the hallway, he moved forward, activating his hat light to blind the camera located at the mid-point of the passage. After he'd gotten by the electronic eye, he toggled the switch, turning off the light just before a middle-aged stoner guy rounded the corner. He didn't make eye contact, instead, he stared down at his phone like most people did, probably looking for dreadlock wax or incense sales as a hippie of his ilk would.

Thank God for those useful distractions, he thought in reference to the smartphone, smiling freely. He didn't have much time; they'd be out of there soon so he needed to move fast. He wedged a wooden door block that was under the bubbler into the bottom crack of the men's room as a means to obstruct its opening should someone be inside. He unzipped his hoodie, revealing a police officer's uniform as the underneath layer. *Get ready, stay on your game. This is an opportunity too rare to squander…*

To his experience, young white girls tended not to

trust a black man. The uniform was leveraged to help erase any of the deep-seated preconceptions about race or general mistrust for strangers that his victims might have. Hershel pulled the metallic aviators from his pocket and threw them on. He clicked the second button on the remote which activated the device he'd set inside the fire alarm. The contraption expanded, causing the lever to be pushed down. The brash, mind-numbing ringing of alarm bells resounded throughout the massive shopping complex, birthing chaos.

Hershel stepped into the emergency exit behind him and peeked out. A larger woman blew out of the bathroom quickly, she mustn't have noticed the door on her way in because she was barreling back down the hallway. Her human fabric apparently of a low moral thread count. Evidently, she only cared about her own ass, giving zero through before bolting away from the frightened children that he knew were inside.

They followed suit seconds after the woman. Hershel saw the twins exit, holding hands. He jerked the exit door open from its cracked state and yelled out, "Hey, kids! Come this way, quick!" while making his uniform fully visible to them. The girls, understanding the situation and seeing his police officer attire, were drawn in. They remembered everything they'd been educated about in school regarding the police and also fire safety, obeying Hershel without hesitation. They jogged down the hallway together before finding the building's exterior.

"Listen, kids, there is a real bad man inside the building, he's been shooting people and killing them. I need you two to stay here for a second, I'm going to bring the car around and get you both back to your parents safely, okay?"

Both of the girls nodded their heads and gave the OK, seemingly terrified by the enriched lies Hershel was varnishing reality with. When he got to his Cadillac, there were still other people funneling out of the building, but thankfully, none from their exit. He whipped up to the curb by the girls and popped the automatic locks for the back doors. The twin in the Coal Chamber shirt speedily pulled open the door handle and they both hustled inside to what they believed to be safety.

BEDLAM

Contradictory to the sensational and publicized breed of killer whose devious smile was inked over every tabloid cover, Hershel had a unique modus operandi. He didn't like to do it himself; his prime desire was simply to watch. It's not that he was squeamish or afraid, he'd just prefer not to touch them. Largely because if he was touching them, he had no way of touching himself.

This odd, incongruous character quirk certainly was fun when it worked but it could also be an annoyance. Arranging a child's slow demise to allow himself to jerk off as he observed was no elementary task. He was like an artist, except he was only painting himself.

His "art" would never be on display to the greater public. His morbid imaginations were confined to the sequestered spaces which only he inhabited. His art could only transpire in the darkest of corners, with

Mephistopheles or equivalent minions by his side. Where they gave him guidance and the breath of their whispers tickled the overgrown hair that protruded from his ears.

The slayings were a lot like television to him, but he perceived them as the absolute highest form of entertainment. A stratum that gave way to a new platform, roughly like a Netflix for the unbalanced. But comparable to television, no viewer desires to keep watching the same show over and over again. We lust for new themes each time. We want them to reach an even more uncomfortable level with new unfolding chapters of perversion.

Like any normal red-blooded American, he wanted the unexpected. He wanted a sharp penetrating notion sinking deep into his bottom lip until it was embedded. He was a fish at the mercy of the angler's hook, destined to be reeled back in before being released only to repeat the same process over in the near future. He wanted insanity. But it should be organic insanity, not forceful—the kind that society acts like we don't want to see yet, secretly, they beg for more of. The major difference was that the show he was producing would never go off the air. The streak would exist for as long as he did. His run was predicated on extreme caution.

The phrase 'variety is the spice of life' was even more applicable when it came to taking a life. A child wasn't exactly an easy commodity to come by... maybe in the Philippines or Honduras they were, but he was in America. The kind of secretive affairs he was immersed in, if found out, would see him executed, if not by the state then by the prisoners of it. It took months and months for him to complete a kidnapping and remain undiscovered. He couldn't bear for each triumph to be peanut butter and jelly every time.

Since he couldn't do it himself, this severely limited his options on approaches that he might potentially be able to consider. He'd had to get more creative with each new murder, otherwise, he'd be doomed to a mundane repetitious progression. This was something he'd started thinking about long before he laid eyes on the twins. He'd been through a slew of ideas already and now his thinking was wandering even further out of left field.

He'd obtained a rather surly African rock python named Mable from a dealer at a reptile expo out in Braintree Mass. The seller was putting a lot of effort into unloading it but was honest about the situation. Apparently, the snake had become increasingly more aggressive and her freshly established attitude problem had, in turn, led to the asphyxiation of the family dog.

He'd raised her from when she could fit in the palm of his hand and now, she was nearly eight feet long and chillingly aggressive. The dealer had kids and feared her continued keeping could create a risk that was high enough to be apprehensive about. Hershel would have kids soon too, but for his purposes, the creature's risk factor was looked at in an auspicious light.

The dreadfulness of the situation spoke volumes to him. Overflowing with enthusiasm after hearing of the hound's demise, he agreed to take the snake off the dealer's hands. The transaction seemed a bit odd to the seller but at the same time, he was just happy to unload the murderous snake. On the ride home from the expo, he couldn't help but think about this confrontational reptile wrapped around the body of a human that it was potentially bigger than. He licked his quivering lips, eager with anticipation as he listened to the serpent slither around in the container behind him.

As he finished reminiscing, his memory transitioned to the present and it was now the twins who were making the noise in the backseat. They'd been asking a lot of questions on the way to meet their parents. Probably because they started to figure out that's not where they were going. They lived in the city where the houses were really on top of each other but now there was only green in their line of sight.

Without a doubt, they'd memorized the route to the mall from their innumerable trips there but wherever this "police officer" was taking them to was foreign, and unrecognizable. The tall trees surrounded them, making the girls feel more claustrophobic but there was not much they could do except wait nervously and see where they were headed.

Hershel pulled onto his far-stretching property which was surrounded in the sort of creepy isolation you might expect from a Vincent Price production. He drove past the house, closer toward the edge of the wide-ranging real estate. He and Madeline were able to afford the eye-catching manor because they were both extraordinarily hard workers. They had the old-school "just get it done and don't complain about it" mentality that humanity was almost unanimously lacking in the current day. It was sorely evident, the shrill-whining hymns of the self-entitled left him on the verge of sickness.

Their lonely late nights and copious hours of mind-numbing overtime had assured that, with their salaries combined, their family would be afforded the rarest luxuries. The class of which many people complained about not having but did nothing to prompt the materialization of. The pool of glamor and indulgence that took a relentless drive and willpower to continue treading water in. So much so, that oftentimes they found themselves too fatigued to enjoy any of it, but that didn't matter; that was just simply who they were.

Once Madeline died, life should have become tighter. She had the higher grossing salary, so it was only natural that they should become more restricted than their glory days. Lucky for Hershel, his wife had taken out a sizable insurance policy, which he was able to collect on. And then, just like the snap of two fingers (or the breaking of a dozen bones and deconstruction of a body), money would no longer be an object for Hershel until he met his own demise.

The imp's sinister blessing shifted Hershel's mental trajectory, ricocheting him back into pondering the thoughts of depravity that had always haunted him. None of the stresses in his life were financial, they were all mental. They all hinged on the untimely death of his soulmate and fathering the three girls that they had created together all by himself. That and, of course, the demons…

Hershel always had these sickening urges ever since he'd learned about sex. In fact, whenever he really thought about his earliest years, he specifically recalled knowing about sex before it was even explained to him. He never could figure out how the images appeared, they were just there.

Even as a child, he knew it seemed strange and he often speculated about his odd origin. Was he really some deranged reincarnation preprogrammed with a corrupt erotic instinct? Does God craft sick ones for fun? The first time he tried playing with himself, they'd emerged even more vibrantly in his mind. They'd been with him forever but now they were truly spreading their wings.

He was thinking about his neighbor, Ms. Becker, who had a habit of oiling up and hanging around outside to sunbathe in her backyard. He'd gotten a peek at her a handful of times already. If he stood on the rim of the bathtub, he was able to look through the bathroom window and see her from a distance. Those were the first feelings of arousal ever generated within him.

A short time later, he was in his bed thinking about an even more scantily clad version of her. There was an eerie obscurity, which looked like a breathing darkness all around her. The nothingness that fenced her in made her pop. She was the only thing that was visible in this auto-piloted fantasy. He wasn't sure exactly what was happening at first, any other self-summoned imagination or daydream he'd found himself in he'd been able to control. Everything he knew about how the brain worked at that age told him that people controlled their fantasies; their fantasies didn't control them…

When the ominous pitch-black backdrop started to illuminate randomly, at first, it disturbed him. But over time, the more that was revealed, the more he enjoyed it. It was like someone was doing flash photography with a high-intensity bulb or flipping a light switch on just to turn it off right afterward. Each time it happened, it offered a glimpse into the savagery, the tortured children in his head. They weren't quite like him; he'd never seen anything like it at the time.

Horrible things were happening to them; they were being cut, ripped, impaled, and violated. The more he saw, the greater his thirst became. Before long, his busty neighbor had been erased from the imaginations altogether and replaced by the young. What was previously a flicker in the background, a mere glimpse at what was hidden was now the dominant norm. He could see everything now, all the time. Hershel had flipped the light switch on completely and once that switch was on, there was no turning it off.

Even though they were both well-off at the time Madeline passed, there is no way she would have signed off on the boat. It was far too expensive, and she was never too big of a water person. It was Hershel that had to influence her to purchase property that was waterfront. There was nothing he enjoyed more than going out on the lake, absent of civilization (and also morality). There was no better drug than the oblivion around them. It was merely him and the playthings he chose to bring along.

It was a good thing that Madeline's opinion wasn't particularly relevant any longer. The insurance policy and her prior inheritance from her mother's passing had been rolled over to him. His most depraved contrivances could now be brought to life, money was merely a formality now. The capital which he used to churn out his repellant brand of selfish pleasantries.

This explained some of his inventions such as the alarm trigger that had assisted him many times in his abduction practices. There were many others. He spent tens of thousands of dollars on his craft. Creating and testing contraptions, of which for their shady potential purposes could never be patented.

That didn't stop him though, his ideas and the advantages they offered were never meant for society. Their only purpose was to aid him in seamlessly acquiring children at a higher but less detectible rate. What began with minor devices evolved into high-quality manufacturing and the finest showpiece of his frightening and dastardly collection: Bedlam.

Bedlam was essentially a small yacht. An Azimut Magellano 66-footer with an interior that Hershel had customized himself. Madeline would have rather put that money towards expensive trips around the globe and other high-brow forms of amusement. Hershel invested it in what, in essence, was a private, sound-proof, floating kill chamber. As a couple, they stood at two very different parts of the prism, to say the least. So, while he missed her, for the most part, he was happy she was gone. Otherwise, his otherworldly assembly would have never existed.

To the few friends he hosted or anyone who ever came aboard that wasn't a target, the boat they set foot on was just a nameless vessel. Something to relax comfortably on while throwing back a few beers. A place of leisure to drop a fishing line from while watching the sun until it dropped out of sight. But to him, during his solitude and, more importantly, to the kids that came aboard, it was Bedlam.

His version of Bedlam, however, was far different than the connotation that his culture associated with the word. For Hershel, the mayhem and turmoil were nothing to be viewed with a negative discernment. In fact, it was everything he'd been dreaming about since he was a child. It was everything he enjoyed about working at the Ladd Institute. It was… everything.

There, within the belly of the boat, was where the devastation occurred. He'd removed all the factory glass that came initially and substituted it with a much thicker sound trapping version. The same went for the walls. To anyone that looked at his interior design, they would be hard-pressed to notice the area where the bed would normally be had been, gutted and replaced with smaller benches that afforded a more spacious design.

The cushioning he'd installed in the lower cabin was also of the noise-absorbing variety. If he was in the undercarriage, someone could be screaming until their lungs split without raising an eyebrow. There could be another boat a few feet away and they wouldn't have the foggiest clue. He'd never even seen another boat on the lake, but in the event that changed, he would be more than prepared.

He had also removed the cream-colored carpet and replaced it with hardwood floors. He knew from his former encounters that killing was ordinarily a messy affair. He regularly draped the kill space with a wide-lipped tarp, but if any fluids were to leak off of it, the carpet would be a much bigger headache than the hardwoods. His most recent finishing touch to the already deceptively ominous room was the glass tank he'd just finished installing.

The tank lined the outskirts of the highest points of the walls in a giant oval shape. Mable, the lethal snake, could now circle the room while watching her soon-to-be-prey squirm with discomfort. She did so under tubes of black-light that stretched the same length, so anywhere she slithered, she was always presenting a supernatural visual. The malevolent hissing serpent glided about, awaiting its release. Anticipating its tender target.

Just like clockwork, that's exactly what she was doing when Hershel brought the twins aboard. They weren't crying yet, but he could tell they were terrified when he'd brandished the machete. He made it very clear to them before they got out of the car that if they didn't follow his exact instructions, they'd be cut up into very small pieces. Hacked and chopped until listening was no longer an option. The heart-pounding and crinkled brow of apprehension turned into body tremors and full-on hysteria when the awestruck twins saw the ghostly reptile.

He slammed the door behind him, trapping the girl's cries inside with him and Mable. He fed on their fear like a fat fuck at an all you can eat buffet. Stuffing his face relentlessly with the rich, creamy screams of their suffering. If it was measured in calories, his strain of gluttony would have left him obese and bedridden long ago. He could spend hours relishing in it, but as much as he wanted to, he was thinking about what came next.

He growled at them like a wicked animal, causing the girls to move a few steps further away from him before he took his seat. "Don't you fuckin' move, don't you fuckin' breathe unless I say so."

The girls responded with compliance, somehow they controlled the bodily functions that had seemed involuntary just seconds ago. He didn't know he'd be bringing two back initially, so he didn't have a ton of time to think about how he would handle the audible. The original plan was to let Mable lethargically crush the lone child he brought back, but now things had become much more interesting. This changed the dynamic entirely, but Hershel felt confident that he could adapt a new method around the previously unforeseen conditions.

There was a handheld power drill holding a five-inch spiral blade that was plugged in beside him. He'd just finished using it a few days earlier when installing Mable's tank. He pulled the trigger of the drill gently, watching it rotate before tossing it on the ground in front of the girls. They stared back up at him confused. The preceding energetic yelping had shifted to silence and now, finally, to a calm sobbing.

"What are your names?" Hershel asked.

The girls took some time before the gothic one stammered out, "H-Hannah."

A few seconds later the athletic sister answered, "Kayla."

"Well, Hannah, Kayla, you both saw how it works, you pull the trigger and it spins," Hershel explained.

"I don't understand, mister, what you want us to do?" Kayla replied, confused by his description.

"If you kill your sister, you don't have to die or, alternatively, if your sister kills you then she doesn't have to die. First one to do it earns the get out of jail free card. The drill is just here to help you."

"Mister, we can't, we can't do that!" Kayla screamed in an attempt to sway his macabre offer. "We're sisters, please don't say that!"

"You'll let us go? I don't believe you." Hannah inquired, through a downpour of tears.

"You can and you will!" Hershel replied sternly in the direction of Kayla. He then turned his attention over to Hannah.

"The reason I can let you go is because I know whoever does the killing won't tell anyone. Because if they did, then everyone would know they were a murderer at that point. They'd be the one going to jail. They'd be the one hated by their parents. Listen, if neither of you choose in the next sixty seconds then my friend, Mable, up there," he pointed to the giant snake, "who's been waiting to hug you since you walked in, will be set free to play with the BOTH of you. It's up to you, it can be one or two…"

Once his longwinded offer concluded, he unzipped himself. He looked at them, terror spilling from their expressions, and began to stroke himself, solidifying from his thoughts of any combination of outcomes. Hershel remained clenching the machete in his left hand, letting them know he was in charge still. He pointed the tip of it toward the power drill, instructing someone to make the move.

"Sixty… fifty-nine… fifty-eight… fifty-seven…"

As his countdown continued, the pressure mounted; the girls were looking at each other and then to the snake. They shrieked as their undeveloped minds tried to calculate which was worse; living with the grief of ending the person they were closest to in the world, or being crushed by an enormous eight-foot python? They both loved each other so dearly, and it was a horrible uncertainty that Hershel had pushed them to face.

"Thirty… twenty-nine… twenty-eight…"

Every five to ten seconds, Hershel would whisper "do it, do it" while he continued to pleasure himself, hoping to motivate one or both of the girls. He was seeing the anxiety elevate more with each tick he called out; they were becoming afraid of each other. Neither of the two was sure if the other had it in them. It wasn't a situation that they could ever have imagined being a part of before setting foot on Bedlam.

Suddenly, Hannah lunged forward and grabbed hold of the drill, struggling to even lift it. Kayla looked at her like her eyes must be deceiving her. Hannah's flimsy wrist was going limp under the weight of the tool, it was all so exhilarating for Hershel.

"Yes, go. GO!" he bellowed out as the veins in his rod bulged.

"Hannah, no, please, what are you doing? Don't, pleeeease!" Kayla cried.

Hannah blocked out the background noise and just tried to focus on the distressing task she'd been forced into. It was difficult enough to attempt it mentally, physically though, it felt impossible. Kayla rushed toward her and knocked the drill out of her hands, letting the heavy equipment fall to the floor.

"What the hell are you doing?!" Kayla screamed in a way that sounded like she'd shredded her throat.

"I have tooooooo…" Hannah blubbered.

"That's right, you have to, bitch. You have to," Hershel whispered, continuing to push buttons.

Hannah bent over and reached for the drill again, but this time, Kayla didn't let her get that far. Being the competitor of the family and an avid soccer player, she launched a kick upward that connected with Hannah's nose and mouth region. A hefty splotch of blood, and the disgorging of the massive greenish-yellow self-supplied swamp of accumulated snot ejected down over the drill and clear tarp. The innumerable tears shed, and stiffness of the blow had created an explosive cesspool of revolting bodily fluids. Hannah sprawled backward onto the floor, landing on her ass motionless and stunned.

It hurt Kayla inside already, the guilt gnawing on her conscience as she reached for the tool. Hannah never really had a chance. While they were similar genetically, Kayla was the only one of the pair to stay active and strengthen her body constantly. The only chance Hannah ever had was catching her by surprise, and that element had already evaporated.

She sat on the stomach of her still-reeling sister, who was disoriented from the unexpected blow. "I'm sorry," Kayla mumbled through a drool-drenched crinkled chin. As the struggling words escaped, it was clear the apology hadn't changed her morbid intent. She held the drill steady from the now-slimy handle, but upside down, driving the heaviest part into her forehead. Up and down, it continued in ruthless fashion. The blows crunched loudly and only died when her sister's movement finally ceased. Kayla gazed down at a bizarre mirror image of her own cracked expression, feeling nauseated.

Hershel was getting close to climax; watching the whole atrocity unfold up close and personal was a perverse treat. "You're not done! Stick it in her, she's still alive! Do it now or you'll get the snake, Kayla! Do it now or you'll regret it, I promise you!"

She hesitated another moment before summoning the wicked courage to move forward with the evil and selfish deed. She pressed the trigger of the tool and closed her eyes, driving it forward as hard as she could. She felt the powerful spiraling bit getting caught up on bone, amongst other mortal tissues.

"HHHHHHHeeeeeeellllllllppppppppuuuuuuggggh hhhhhaaa!" Hannah moaned out like she'd just woken up on fire. "Whhhhhhhhhhhhhhhhhhhyyyyyyyy!"

"I'm sorry! I'm sorry, Hannah!" Kayla screamed, disturbed by the noises she was emitting. Hannah didn't stop. When Kayla opened her eyes, she could see the drill spinning half deep into her sinus cavity while the blood and booger splattered all around. She was teetering closer to insanity due to the length of the appalling chore; mania now boiling within her as she manipulated the twisting steel to dance up and down.

"JUST DIE! JUST FUCKING DIE PLEASE!" she shrieked, removing the running instrument out of the pulverized nasal crater and instead, substituting it for her eyeball. She pushed down with all of her might, causing the flood of gore to explode out of the socket. Hershel exploded right along with Hannah's face and let out a satisfied sound of deep relief.

Kayla felt the gore-filled grooves of the devilish drill-bit rubbing up against the whittling arches of her orbital bone as Hannah lost all movement. The fight was finished, her breathing was no more.

Kayla was spent, drained both physically and emotionally, scarred forever. She felt a strange hunger and queasiness come over her before a lightheaded feeling of disorientation. As she collapsed into the puddle of hot red and mucus that surrounded her dead sister, the last thing she saw was what she'd done. The primal deconstructed face that used to tell her secrets and jokes was now just a bloody memory.

***

When Kayla awoke, she was inside the hospital laying on an elevated bed. Her mother and father sat by her side as she started to regain her awareness. They stood over her so thankful that their little darling was safe and sound but also visibly entrenched in the pitfall of a cavernous separate concern. The prodding anguish was unmistakably imprisoned within their pupils. They were no doubt waiting for her to explain to them what she knew about Hannah's whereabouts. After getting her bearings back and talking with her parents a few moments, she started to remember the blasphemy she'd committed.

She recalled each savage strike that beat her kind face into a state of senselessness. She remembered the spiraling drill-tip burrowing inside her to a finality that was beyond life-altering. She remembered the ruby outpouring of her beloved doppelganger's youthful essence, running out like a busted pipe. The last horrid image of her inverted nasal basin and her former functioning eye socket that had been left a disturbing gore pool.

As it all came rushing back, she began to rush away from it. She knew Hershel was right; there was no earthly way that she could explain what she'd done to her sister. She'd left her best friend, her own flesh and blood, a muddled heap of chewed up humanity. It wasn't prison that scared her as much as how they would look at her; she felt incredibly alone and riddled with irreparable damage.

"Where's Hannah?" she asked, not knowing what else to say. To her, acting like she didn't remember was so much better than the truth. It was the only option to avoid getting trapped in her own lies.

Her mother and father looked at them with crushing grief and disappointment. They buried it well enough that she wouldn't have known it was there if she didn't know the truth. Her mother was biting her lip so hard she was just short of drawing blood. She held back the tears with everything she had.

Before either of them could respond to answer her question, a nurse entered the room. "Oh, thank heavens you're finally awake, how wonderful. We just have a few more tests we need to run and then after that, the police will need to ask Kayla a few questions. Mom and Dad, would that be okay? Would you mind coming with me for just a couple of minutes? Then I promise you can see her as long as you'd like."

They both nodded solemnly and rose to their feet

as Kayla's eyes begged them to stay. "Mom, Dad, wait, can't they just stay?"

"Honey, I promise they will be back in a jiffy. Dr. Guyver will be in to see you in just a moment, dear, sit tight," the sweet-voiced nurse reassured her. She escorted her folks out of the examination room and further down the hall, closing the door behind them.

It didn't even take thirty seconds before he popped his round head inside, bearing a strange grimace. There was something different about him from the other doctors that Kayla had seen during her typical physicals and regular office visits. He was a lot more disheveled and poorly groomed. He was outfitted in a raggedy white coat that was soiled with mucky smears. Even his stethoscope looked filthy; a build of orange wax sat atop the set of formerly snowy earbuds.

"So, how are you feeling now?" Dr. Guyver inquired, his accent sounded thick and German.

"I feel sick," Kayla replied dejectedly.

"Well, let us see if we can figure out what's wrong then, okay sweetie?"

She nodded her head as he approached her, placing the crusted and gooey stethoscope into his hairy ears. He guided it gently over her heart and listened to it pound rapidly. His eyebrows seemed confused as they mushed together. He dropped the drum down from her sternum and looked back up at her.

"Maybe if you don't kill your sister, you feeling much better," he explained while his accent funneled out an even more broken variety of English.

A spine-tingling terror jolted her up off the hospital bed, her eyes overflowing with shock. *How could he know? It wasn't possible!* her mind screamed.

Dr. Guyver quickly wrapped both of his large dirty

hands around her tiny throat and started to choke her with a menacing expression stamped upon him.

A bright blinding light started to cut through her now-closed eyes. The air was exiting her body, running free and fast without looking back. Through the white mystical illumination, another picture began to steadily emerge. She also felt an additional crushing sensation of pressure running down the rest of her body, not just where Dr. Guyver had his hands.

As the light started to flicker, the real picture finally became frighteningly vibrant. She was confronted by Hershel's creepy cutting glare again, succumbing to the perversion he desired so deeply as he watched Mable's fat body worm its way around hers. She'd awoken for certain this time stunned, having been tricked during her slumber, leaving one nightmare to enter an even more terrifying one. The air supply inside her torso was becoming more of a commodity by the second.

Crimson coated the snake's slick back as it tightened the crushing vice-grip on her minuscule frame. Kayla's vision became obscured by the cracking blood vessels in her eyes. She could feel them individually bursting one by one. She wanted to scream but it was no longer possible. The last thing she saw was Hershel's yellow-toothed smile speaking the final words she would hear.

"I had my fingers crossed."

TEENAGE
TREPIDATION

The uncomfortable angst had been all too prominent since the talks of their future had suddenly arisen. Jesse had been dating Noah since the seventh grade. They might not have been the most popular couple at Bend Brook High, but they were by far the most consistent. No one had been going steady longer or appeared so picturesque.

Oh, Noah, what are we gonna do? she wondered to herself. Her fingers gently traced over an old photo of them at Wendy's. It was taken just days after they'd first met. *I'm gonna miss that dorky smile…*

Noah and Jesse were both artistic in different ways but alike in the sense that they were staunchly driven. They shared pores that permeated with passion. Jesse had been experimenting with make-up effects since she was a kid, and for her, the curiosity really all tied back to Halloween. Her passion for horror was cultivated from a young age. While her peers were figuring out new ways to look cute, she was pondering the opposite; how to appall everyone she came into contact with.

Watching the crude killers slowly slay their victims, and creatures mutate into bubbling monstrosities wasn't anything that had ever come close to scaring her. She always understood it wasn't real but still suspended her disbelief enough to engross herself in the weird yet wonderful world of horror.

What fascinated her even more than watching the nasty murders and bone-crushing monsters were how they did it. How did Bob Bottin make the monster in *The Thing* or the werewolves in *The Howling* look so convincing? If she could pick anyone's brain in the horror business, it would have to be Bob Bottin or Tom Savini. Tom's work was phenomenal and stretched back decades and decades with humbling consistency. Whether it was the kill scenes in *The Prowler*, or the strange blob-like lake monster in *Creepshow 2*, or masterminding his own exploding skull in *Maniac*, any true student of cinematic violence knew that the gore and realism didn't get much better than Tom Savini.

That's why in exactly two years she'd be heading to Monessen Pennsylvania for a while to attend Tom's very own special effects school. Why the hell else would anyone journey to a place named Monessen? She'd been daydreaming about it for years; envisioning her rapid development. Moving on from her own entertaining, but amateur work that she'd become known for, and evolving into someone who could hopefully be a competent hand on the set of the next great slasher.

She'd made a few short films herself with friends that were pretty special to her. One was called *The Black Shit* and was about a jogger who came across a homeless vagrant living in a shack in the woods. He happened to be dripping with some black slimy life form which he, predictably, would then transfer to the jogger. The process of making The Black Shit itself was more than enjoyable—to her, it was heaven. It required a lot of cornstarch, patience, and black food coloring (which was surprisingly expensive!). Now if only she could get paid to do it…

Jesse was a death rocket fueled by enthusiasm. She was born ready to get her feet wet with corn syrup, fake innards, and chunky steaming vomit. She was designed to mortify and unravel the undeveloped, vulnerable psyches of children watching movies they shouldn't well past their bedtime.

Quite, in clear contrast to her devout views, stood her partner. Noah, an artist himself, could never be seduced by horror or the vintage style special effects that captivated Jesse. He was a theater buff that fashioned himself as the next Daniel Day Lewis but was probably a lot closer to the next Jeff Daniels. Which would be an awesome thing to most people but ironically not to Noah. He was confident at least, he really believed his own bullshit, which in some ways attracted Jesse.

She hated the theater and HATED musicals in particular; sitting through them felt like nails on a chalkboard. But that was Noah's creative outlet. She always pushed him and supported him despite their opposing interests. Supposedly, he had a potential opportunity at the Lee Strasburg Theater and Film Institute in New York. It would be a great place for him to develop and hone his craft while also giving him a high probability of finding some immediate work post-graduation.

New York and Pennsylvania weren't terribly far apart but Jesse was well aware of how these sorts of situations tended to play out. People go to different schools, develop cliques, hang out with other members of the opposite sex, and boom! You've fallen out of love with a person just as quickly as you fell into it. It was only natural in her eyes; people want to be with a partner they can be around, especially young people.

The nature of the beast was such a tragic and heart-mashing one, but the more she thought about it, maybe it wouldn't be the worst thing in the world. While she supported Noah on his dull ventures into realms that disinterested her, Noah was the reverse. He enjoyed nitpicking her attraction to the evil niche genre. It was something she was starting to tire from hearing about. His advice could be highly obnoxious at times.

He felt that the horror, in general, couldn't be taken seriously. That there would be no "meaningful" films presented from a group who saw dollar signs in the most juvenile butchery. A community that only existed to prey on people's fears with mysterious monsters and bait randy teens with movies that promised to be littered with cheap nudity and sex appeal. He couldn't understand that ugly can be pretty, and that sleazy can be sexy, even beautiful in some instances. In her opinion, unconventional didn't always translate to unsuccessful.

He constantly tried to steer Jesse into CGI or computer effects, concluding (with his "expert" opinion) that it was the only way of the future for entertainment. Jesse saw the retro effects from her own unique perspective. To her, it had nothing to do with the future of effects, it was only about the past. It was what she loved and appreciated growing up; it was like records or used clothing.

The retro would always resurface eventually. People needed nostalgia to remember who they were and what they came from. It was the very fabric and foundation that had established their current day character. The automobile wouldn't be at all impressive if it wasn't for the horse and carriage. There would always be a place for the past and if there wasn't, in time, the people would demand it.

Even if, for some reason, people never revolted against the cookie-cutter digitized mess that in her opinion felt too larger than life, she'd still be content with her choice. The real stuff that you could physically feel was all that she wanted. She needed to craft the puppets, sculpt the latex, and mix the blood herself. She wouldn't be able to rest in her grave if she didn't find a way to accomplish it.

Noah, for all of his faults, could still be the sixteen candles special. Jesse got to see a side of him that only flashed behind closed doors. It made her feel loved and special. No one else knew about the guy who made a necklace for her using a rock from the beach they fell in love on. Most other boys in their age group would be pounding beers and trying to compare belt notches with each other. He was much more mature in his own right. That's the part of him she treasured. She'd been able to swallow the snooty know-it-all percentage of his personality in exchange to continue on with the starry-eyed one.

It would hurt if they were unable to keep it going but that was still some time away. She figured that finishing up the junior year together and having some enchanting memorable moments as seniors was the most important thing. Even if they didn't pan out afterward, they could look back on those simple carefree times with a warm feeling. They could both know that they found love and companionship in each other during a period where most didn't.

She already knew the most important aspect of her adolescent remembrances was going to be the Skeleton Un-formal. It was Bend Brook High's yearly dance to celebrate the macabre and ghastly. The dance occurred every autumn and was now merely a week away. Convincing Noah to put aside his sneering criticism of her favorite holiday had been a chore in itself, but with or without him she was going. He knew how much it meant to her but still did everything he could to try and worm his way out of attending it.

She took the greatest pride of all in her costume creation. She'd won the best costume award two years in a row and felt that earning the nomination every year of high school was like her rite of passage. She'd pulled off a remarkable Linda Blair replication, pea soup puke and all last year. The wounds and discoloration were particularly realistic and her possessed portrayal was methodical. The contest wasn't really that, no one else was close to that level of dedication and detail.

Now she was set to take on a less iconic but more challenging character. She would be the partially-mutated version of Natasha Henstridge from the sci-fi horror thriller *Species*. She already had the blonde hair and the sort of rectangular face that Henstridge had, so it was a natural fit. She'd been working on the suit all year long. The alien skin was looking more like a living organism with each passing week.

The mutated arm slipped on and fit perfectly. The slightly slimy, long sharp nails and jade complexion felt out of this world. The mask she'd been working on would cover about a quarter of her face, representing the partial mutation with a faultless balance.

She would mesh it in with the latex she planned to hand-paint, which would give it the authentic movie set feel. She was never one to pat herself on the back but as she moved on from the tattered photograph and refocused on inspecting her work, she found her detail and craftsmanship to be nearly impeccable. It seemed apparent that she'd have another accolade certificate and Dunkin' Donuts gift card in no time.

Noah eventually realized that if he didn't go to the dance with Jesse, she'd never forgive him. He'd trotted over to the local Spirit of Halloween and settled on a dime-a-dozen asylum worker outfit. It didn't have any heavy make-up involved and was comfortable, which was essentially all he cared about. While Jesse wasn't enthralled with the choice, she was glad he was trying, even if he was half-assing it.

Jesse sat at her table hands caked in dry paint and other creative materials, meticulously applying a few final strokes to her soon-to-be face-for-a-night when, suddenly, the door opened up.

Her father popped his head inside and smiled at her, "Noah's outside."

"Thanks, Dad! Tell him I'll be down in just a minute."

"Wow some pretty creepy stuff in here, *Species* was the perfect pick. You look just like her you know. Heck, what am I saying, you're a lot prettier than her," he complimented, overly proud of his daughter for more reasons than he could count.

"Dad, you're making me blush," she replied sheepishly.

"Really though, this stuff looks great, Jess. I couldn't be more impressed by the things you come up with. I just hope you'll come and take care of me still when you're all famous in a few years. You aren't gonna forget about us small-timers, right?"

"I'm not gonna be famous but I will *still* come back and change your diapers in a few years regardless, I promise, okay?"

"It's a deal."

Jesse washed her hands in the bathroom before snatching up her handbag and racing down the stairs. "Love you, Mom, love you, Dad!" she yelled out without stopping as she exited, closing the screen door. Noah was sitting in his mom's white Fiat 500, but the car seemed to suit someone of his character. The apple didn't fall too far from the tree.

The foliage around them looked gorgeous, it was as bright as the candy corn that no one ate. Much of it was still on the trees but a sizable amount lay draped over the sidewalks. As she took a seat in the car, she was already regretting not bringing a sweater. The cool, crisp weather had been on an incline. There wouldn't be too many more nights you could be comfortable without an extra layer or two.

That was the one thing about Halloween that was trying; sometimes costumes called for a lack of apparel. If you'd selected a costume of that nature then you'd be tortured by the chills the entire evening. To Jesse, in some cases, the sacrifice could be worth it. But she wasn't the type to use the holiday as a dress like a skank for a night pass. Those girls were the ones that really suffered.

"Well, aren't you looking sexy today? I love it when you wear those Lucky jeans."

"Why thank you, you're not so bad yourself," Jesse said, batting her eyes and then giving him a peck on the cheek.

He fired up a joint and took a couple of deep pulls before passing it over to Jesse. "So, I was thinking we could do sushi if you're cool with that?" he asked, eyes still sifting through the orangey leaves breezing through the road.

"Definitely, I want something that I can eat a fuckload of and still feel light. Where you thinking though?"

"How about that new place over on the Eastside? What's it called, Tokyo Express?"

"I didn't even know there was a new spot, where on the Eastside is it?"

"Yeah, it literally just launched last week. Cheryl and Paul said it was fuckin' unbelievable. It's just a couple blocks past the Ladd Institute."

"That seems like a really weird place for a restaurant, but I guess crazy people like sushi too…"

Noah laughed at the notion, creating a strange image in his head of madmen struggling to pinch rolls with chopsticks. "It's not like they let them out for lunch just because they're in the vicinity, although that would be amazing."

"Right? We can always dream I guess."

THE NEW GUY

Even on the first day you meet someone, it's not difficult to get a feel for them. The old expression about first impressions had always held true for Hershel. Lawrence was a bit of an oddball, the scrawny, fidgety type that never quite seemed sure of himself. Which is why it struck Hershel as strange that he'd taken a job at the Ladd Institute; a facility that was well known for housing some of the most violent and deranged individuals in the tiny state of Rhode Island.

You could go on about the collection of evil within and all their sins for eternity. You had Craig Price, the Warwick slasher who'd decimated a woman with a butcher knife at the tender age of just thirteen before assimilating seamlessly back into ordinary everyday life. He'd resurface two years later, slaughtering another woman along with her nine and eleven-year-old daughters. He'd completely caved in one child's skull and stabbed the trio so many times that the knife blade had snapped off from the handle completely. He was sick but not the sickest…

Michael Woodmansee was also a depraved example of the horrors within the walls of the institute. When he was just sixteen, he'd strangled a five-year-old that lived in his neighborhood, stripped his bones of the flesh, and shellacked his little skeleton. He kept a depraved journal that was allegedly so horrific it was deemed unfit for public consumption. The speculation and rumor had indicated that he'd eaten him. His father was a policeman which probably helped him avoid suspicion to some extent. Luckily for the small city of Woonsocket, he was caught in the act of his attempted follow-up murder before anyone else died or was cannibalized.

Even in the smallest state of the country, there were dark corners all around. Those fellas were just the warm-ups, things got far worse from there. Hershel understood exactly why he was there. If his guise was ever lifted, he would quickly be promoted from employee to customer. He was just exceptionally good at keeping secrets and covering tracks, that was the biggest variance. It was what separated the sick fucks standing outside the cell from the ones trapped within it. But the real question was, did Lawrence understand why he was there?

If it was just for a paycheck, that would be a choice he'd live to regret. Hershel knew a man had to be built a certain way and have a rigid enough callus to simmer in a frying pan with the worst of the worst. You're not just giving in a place like Ladd, the institute is also taking. Each day you broke the threshold, a part of you died and the sanity level of all inside (those there by choice or otherwise) took a baby step closer to aligning. The titles and semantics didn't matter, they all had too much in common.

Lawrence, at the very least, lacked that callus; his demeanor just screamed coward. The moment he saw him, he thought about how he resembled a dog with its tail everlastingly stuck between its legs. Today would be an interesting day, it's not often that Hershel got to watch someone ingest the degeneracies housed in the decaying old building for the first time. He'd already given him a speedy tour and went over the layout. The basics that were provided to every employee regardless of their occupation.

Next, they'd moved onto the less ordinary aspects of the day-to-day. He'd introduced him to the more popular and sensationalized subjects that sat confined to their dark cells, mumbling nonsense to whoever might be willing to listen. Those subjects were always entertaining but not quite as fun as others. Hershel found the ones with stories that hadn't been beaten to death by the press to be even more intriguing. The unknown evils that might have been living next door and you'd never even know it.

The forgottens and throwaways. The scarce few that were outcast by society and forced into the wickedest of solitude. He had access to all the bizarre minute details of their lives. From the most heinous of their atrocities to the gloomy unnoticed injustices committed against them. He had the information to understand just how criminal they actually were.

There was one man in particular that he'd been obsessing over for some time now. He was hardly a complex character but, in his eyes, the irony of his tale spoke to him. He was fascinated with how the barbarity of life's lessons had contorted him into a walking slaughterhouse. An imbalanced, frightening picture that people forgot to mention at church when praising God for his many beautiful creations. It was time to show him Edmon…

As they approached the cell door, Hershel leaned up against the cold wall and lit a Newport. He was holding a rather bulky file in one hand and then lit tobacco in the other. Lawrence had a befuddled look come over him, jaw jumping a few times before he assembled the sack to spit out his question.

"We can smoke in here?"

"Why do you ask? Do you smoke Lawrence?" Hershel inquired.

"Well, no, bu—"

"Then what the fuck do you care? Do as I say, not as I do, can you remember that for me?"

"Yes, I can remember that."

"That's good, 'cause otherwise, I promise you, they'll eat your ass alive in here. You work here long as I did, and you'd be fuckin smokin' too. I don't need you preachin' to me," he scolded, now blowing his exhale in Lawrence's face intentionally. Hershel just eyeballed him for a few seconds, letting his hateful glare resonate, ensuring that he understood talk like that directed toward him wouldn't go over as easily next time.

"So, listen, I brought you here—now that we have the basics out of the way—because I need you to understand exactly what you're getting into. All the stuff you've seen so far, while it's horrible and disturbing, it ain't shit. It's the ones you ain't seen or heard about that you need to primarily concern yourself with. The element of surprise is one of their most valuable tools. It's also one of the deadliest." He pulled in another deep hit and looked in through the small rectangle slit on the cell door.

"Okay, I'm listening, Mr. Hughes."

"Good, took you long enough. I suggest you pay close attention because this is when you find out if you have what it takes."

"I already know I have what it ta—"

"You don't know shit, son! All you know is that you're here. That you had the nuts to fill out a little piece of fuckin' paper and get you an interview so you could take a walk around. You ever seen a decapitated body?"

"What?"

"A fuckin' dead body with the head ripped off, you ever seen that shit?"

"No, no sir, Mr. Hughes."

"Well, that's just one flavor of the type of shit you're gonna taste in here. Let me tell you, this place ain't just some paperwork or sitting at a desk. This place is hell. I should know, I've been working here for over three decades, you understand me?"

"Yes, sir."

"You ever heard the name Edmon Black before?"

"No, is he a transfer?" Lawrence asked, trying to peer through his side of the opening.

"No, more of a forgotten local legend. His life was the type of situational satire that Shakespeare dreamed about. If you ever wanna know what insomnia feels like, his case file would be an ideal read."

"How many people did he kill?"

They both stared solemnly into the cell at the hulking figure sitting in the corner and staring at the wall. His shaved head bumpy and grooved with deformity. A bluish hue cast over the dark cell, the lighting made Lawrence's first gaze especially creepy. The sound of flapping skin coincided with his air intake. A chill shot straight through Lawrence's body. If Hershel was trying to scare him, he was doing an impeccable job. The off-putting gesture sustained at a steady pace while their conversation continued.

"It's not about a number, it's about how he got there. His story started even before he was born."

"Why does he sound like that? It's, ugh, disgusting," Lawrence scoffed.

"Son, if you're disgusted by that then its best I don't answer the question."

"No, I'm sorry, forget I said anything. I really want to know more about the patients. I'll keep all my criticisms to myself."

"It would certainly behoove you to, considering you might have to step in that cell with him one day."

Lawrence's stare drifted off Hershel and back into the cell while he listened intently to his tale, picturing it with a series of vivid mental stills.

"His mother wasn't the most beautiful woman but by all accounts, a nice keep-to-yourself kind of lady. She had trouble finding a man and was just about over the hill, so, she decided to be artificially inseminated. If she wasn't going to have a man in her life, she at least wanted a child.

Hershel took another deep drag of the smoke, closing his left eye momentarily before continuing. "Everything was going great and she was only a short while from her due date when she got the call. The clinic that had helped her conceive explained to her that the man who was her donor had executed his family in horrific fashion, and on top of that, had gone missing... Being that she took in his seed, they were apparently fearing for her life with him on the run."

"Holy shit. Wait, aren't most of those types of programs private? How would he even know how to find her?" Lawrence inquired.

"Very good, Lawrence, did you ever try getting pregnant? You sure seem to know a lot about this."

"No, I just—I—someone told me about it is all…" he stammered, presenting like he was obviously trying to cover something up.

"Right… well the confidentiality wasn't applicable in this case because someone had broken into the clinic and stolen the records, presumably the donor."

"No, way."

"So, it turns out while she was on the phone with the clinic, receiving this news, the donor was already in the house. He put a power drill through her pregnant stomach that shredded it. Edmon's fetal throat, chin, and vocal cords were violently ripped up in the cycling steel. Mangled beyond repair."

As Hershel recanted the story, he couldn't help but think about the situation on Bedlam with the twins. Did he simply choose the drill because it was randomly lying there, or was he subconsciously motivated by Edmon's tragic past?

"So that's why he sounds like that every time he takes a breath?" Lawrence queried.

"That's right, and that's why, eventually, when you see his face, you'll never forget it."

"That's sick. But it still doesn't explain how he wound up in here though," Lawrence prodded him, now hungry for extra details.

"Well it turns out, the doctors surmised that if she hadn't been pregnant, the drill would have split her main artery and she'd have expired long before she ever reached the hospital. Paradoxically, if she hadn't been with child in the first place, the donor would have never even had her in his crosshairs. Think about that for a second…"

Hershel drew a deep, final drag from his smoke and opened his bloodshot eyes wildly, "The police shot the deranged donor and Edmon's mom more than finished the job, but she got stuck living out the prime years of her life beside a nightmare. A monstrosity that had suicide seeming more appealing to her by the day."

Hershel dropped the remaining filter to the floor and stepped on it, then twisted his foot over the butt. "It was a miracle he even survived, probably a miracle his mother wished God wouldn't have performed."

"Why's that?"

"Well, since he was born early, he'd succumb to severe brain damage, that's why he can't speak. And look at the size of him. No baby born prematurely looks like this. They're usually feeble, only able to live on with the assistance of machines. Not Edmon though, he's something else. It's hard to tell and you probably wouldn't notice unless you'd been around him as long as I have, but you'll eventually notice he has a strange artic skin pigment. It's subtle, doesn't jump out at you. Makes him look like he's been sitting in a freezer his whole life. Like he's dead almost."

"I don't get it. If he was born prematurely then why's he so, so, massive? Like you said, with the circumstances, it doesn't really make sense."

"It does if you read the file. The doctors essentially were confronted with a decision. One which they had to make on behalf of the parents. His mother was incapacitated and in surgery, his father at the time was, we'll just say inaccessible. They were tasked with making a major medical decision on behalf of the parents."

Hershel opened up the thick file that he'd been carrying with him. "Again, these should be your best friends in here, I can't stress that enough. You can find out the details of all of these animals. We have access to their histories, even the lesser-known aspects… I suggest you learn them, memorize them like your future depends on it otherwise you'd be doing yourself a grave disservice. I could sit here and tell you about the people that didn't learn them and how short-lived and unrewarding their lives became, but I think you get the idea."

"Don't worry, after this story, I'll definitely be reading those. If not for my own safety, then just purely for my entertainment. This story is fucking nuts." Lawrence conceded, making a detailed mental note. "So, what was the medical decision?"

He pointed with his finger onto the paper and cited a few paragraphs of information. "So, as you can see here, his heart had stopped. Normally that's the end of the road but at that time there was a, let's call it, a controversial option."

"Well, what was it?"

"You ever heard of Brinemax?"

"The sewage disposal people?"

"No, what would that have to do with this? Jesus, they're a pharmaceutical slash alternative medicine company out West in Arizona. From what the case file says, at this time, they'd partnered with a handful of hospitals around the country to supply them with an experimental drug. Some kind of adrenaline and steroid concoction. If it's administered within a few minutes of death, they speculated it had the ability to bring them back. So, when mommy and daddy are away, the doctors will play."

"But obviously it worked."

"It did, yes, but it also nearly killed him. His muscle mass increased to such a point of inflation that it nearly ripped through his skin. In fact, as a baby, he had to be sewn up religiously as he was constantly outgrowing himself. It was incredibly painful for poor Edmon. He was just splitting at the seams all the way up until adulthood. I've seen the scars that cover his body. He looks like a human jigsaw puzzle. You can imagine why he might have developed a temper, living in constant agony, every waking moment was hell. You'll understand soon when you see his face, you'll know that it's not meant to be on a man walking upright. It's the kind you don't see because they already closed the casket."

"But it's better than being dead, right?"

"The medical board didn't seem to think so; the treatment was ordered to be discontinued immediately. All remaining supply of the drug was said to have been destroyed shortly after the grueling side-effects were discovered. Edmon was the one and only recipient— the gift and the curse all wrapped up together for you. So, better than being dead? Lawrence, I assure you, if working here does one thing for you, it will be helping you realize that there are so many things worse than death."

Hershel closed the file and drew his attention back into the cell. "In all the years he's been here, no one has ever been able to communicate with him. This was exactly how he was at his mother's house. Just walking around, this empty imbecile void of any common human traits except for the deeply embedded, almost instinctual, love that he had for his mother."

"Poor lady, she thought she'd finally have someone to spend her life with and the doctors end up creating this freak."

"Exactly, and the attack left her wheelchair bound, so the simplest life tasks became challenging for her. The report discusses how it became risky for anyone to come to the house. Edmon would become highly agitated and eventually confrontational with them for no reason at all. He's was territorial—like a dog—when it came to his house and his mother. The attacks were so violent that his mother was forced to lock him in his room, similar to what you're looking at right now really. His whole life has seen him confined, regardless of his location. It's all he really knows."

"That still doesn't explain why he's here, did he kill the people he attacked?"

"I'm getting to it. Be patient, damn it," Hershel commanded coldly.

"Sorry."

"It was nothing that extreme until his 27th birthday. A man showed up at the door, allegedly from the clinic that helped his mother conceive. He asked to come inside and talk with her. She allowed it, curious as to why anyone from the fuckin' sperm bank of all places would be getting in touch so far after the fact. He explained that he was the one that called her on that fateful day of the attack. He told her that he was sick, a twisted pervert. He said that he'd forged the donor name on her paperwork."

"What?" Lawrence replied, dumbfounded and on the edge of his seat.

"It was his semen that was in the tube, not the man,

who, oh by the way, just happened to be an absolute fuckin' maniac, that he'd randomly chosen to put down her form. He was a donor, but not her donor."

"Christ, this thing has more twists than a bag of peppermints."

"Well, there ain't anything refreshing about this one, it only gets more sour from there. So, his real father, the man from the clinic is there, only out of decades of guilt, and he really has no idea what Edmon has transformed into. He only knows that he's never met his son and it's finally time to."

"Yeaaaaaah, and?"

"So, he goes into his bedroom where his mom had him locked, and right when he steps foot inside, she slams the door shut and traps him. It didn't take long for Edmon to get started on him. He pulled his heart out of his chest with his bare hands and ripped it in half like a piece of paper. He folded his father's spine in a way that made the expression bending over backwards all too literal. I've seen the photo, shit is no exaggeration, he made that mother fucker look like the McDonald's arch. His strength is just ridiculous."

"Man, that's… intense."

"It's more than that, that wasn't even the end of it. Eventually, the police show up and try to take custody of Edmon but he ended up killing three cops before being shot seventeen times. The lone survivor from the initial unit on the scene said he had to actually reload after dumping a full clip in him before he dropped. Yet again, somehow, against all odds, he survived…"

"How did he kill the three cops?" Edmon turned his head slightly to the side, offering a brief snapshot of the pulverized, muddled meat that dominated his expression. His strait-jacket appeared uncomfortably tight. It was like his body type created clothing dimensions not yet conceived, but still, there it clung, spray-painted over his enormous frame. Lawrence shuddered and looked away just as Hershel thought he might.

"Crushed bones, torn flesh, detached limbs, eyes gouged, and of course, decapitations, hence my earlier inquiry with you." Hershel flashed a smirk for the first time all night.

"Wow, this is the kind of guy you'd never want to escape. I mean, can you imagine seeing this fucker strolling around the grocery store? I'd probably shit myself on the spot," Lawrence confided.

Something clicked in Hershel's head. A brilliant idea that fed into his own hidden crudeness was just served up to him on a silver platter. "Wait, what did you just say?" he asked, not believing he hadn't thought of it himself already.

"I said, this is the kind of guy you would never want to escape. How can you rehabilitate that level of savagery? This isn't Canada. It sounds like his mother was probably the only person he wouldn't harm." Hershel still stood in awe of the concept, piecing it together in his mind.

"You know, like in the movies, you always hear about the maniac escaping from the asylum, usually around Halloween, like right now? It's like the most rehashed storyline in existence but, somehow, it never gets old, to me anyway. Then they always go on a killing spree, massacring hordes of horny kids. It's fun to watch I guess, but when you consider the real thing with someone like this…"

"Yeah, I've seen that movie, it never does get old. If you want some eyeballs, all you need is sex and death. It's a guaranteed draw every time." Hershel half answered while his mind dabbled in the fantasy that was being put forth.

"I mean, just look at his face, it even looks like a costume. It doesn't even fuckin' look real," Lawrence explained, conveying what he'd observed a bit earlier.

Hershel still had a sinister grin carved out from his lips when he turned his full attention over to Lawrence. He patted him on the back a couple of times, keeping his pupils connected.

"You know, maybe I was wrong about you, Lawrence. Maybe I jumped the gun a little bit. I think you just might be cut out for this place after all…"

TOKYO EXPRESS

Jesse and Noah sat with their shoes off and legs folded at the traditional miniature chabudai tables. People usually enjoyed sitting at them when they wanted to get a more authentic dining experience. They picked at the remainder of the trinity of rolls they'd selected. Neither liked eel as they were unable to get the thought of the creature slithering around, fangs readied, out of their heads. They'd tried it previously but both had settled on the safer selections of Yellowtail and jalapeno, Philadelphia and California rolls.

Noah unhinged his chopsticks and latched onto the Philadelphia roll, eyeing its cream cheese content. "Philadelphia, so how close is that from… where is it? Monessen?" he asked judgingly.

"Not as close as you'd think. It's like five hours or something," Jesse replied, ignoring his jab.

"I don't understand why you won't just consider

New York, they have some of the best Houdini certified CGI schools in the country. That's where the future of filmmaking is at, Jesse, that's where the money is going to be. I don't understand why you don't trust me on this, my uncle Norman actually has contacts in the industry. He's got over twenty years of total experience. This is not just some hypothesis, it's solid, plus, we could still be together."

"Let me ask you a question. Did anyone at those schools have their heads explode like a watermelon while sitting at lover's lane?"

"What?"

"Did any of them have a gun fixed to their crotch where the barrel was the shaft and two cylinders were the balls?"

"What in hell are you talking about?"

"Tom Savini, Noah! My idol. Those were roles he played in Maniac and From Dusk 'Til Dawn, but you can't seem to understand that. You don't understand me! I don't care about CGI and the "future of film" or what your fucking industry insider uncle says! Have you just not been paying attention to anything I've said, like for my whole life?" She'd finally blown a gasket.

Noah sat, blood rushing to his cheeks. He'd never seen this kind of conviction expel from her. Two old ladies that were at a sit-down table in the other room peered over in their direction.

"I don't think I can do this anymore, you just… you don't get it, Noah." She stormed off consuming all of the mic time before he could even get a word in.

The bite of sushi that was pinched between Noah's sticks fell down, smacking into the saucer of soy sauce and splashing some on him. Seconds later, Jesse was back. She'd realized that she was shoeless and returned to retrieve her vans. They were slip-ons, so Noah knew he didn't have much time. He got up from the table and wrapped his arms around her.

"I'm sorry, Jess. I listen to you, I promise I do. You're right, it's wrong for me to try and pressure you into a professional future. While I do believe the things I said to be true, I understand you have a passion. The financial aspects aside, I want you to do what makes you happy. I'll never bring up CGI again, I swear."

"You mean it?" she asked still a bit unsure of his sincerity.

"I promise, I just want what's best for you AND what's best for me. I know being able to see you in person is best for me, but I understand how important Morrison is to you."

"Monessen."

"Right, Monessen. Maybe I can… maybe I can take a look around Pennsylvania and see what kind of schools there are. Maybe it's me that should be taking an initiative instead of trying to push you into one."

"Noah, I don't expect you to sacrifice New York for me."

"What if I wanted to?"

She moved in closer and kissed him deeply, their tongues mingled with the kind of teenage enthusiasm that only lasts for a short window in one's life. They pulled away, looking at each other with those googly-eyes that only our youthful innocence can produce. They hugged tightly again for a moment, not caring what others thought about their spat, before finally prying themselves apart.

"So, are you gonna have your Species costume ready to Rock & Roll? Halloween is just a week away," Noah reminded her.

"You know it, I'm even better when I'm under pressure. Somebody's gotta win this contest three years in a row, right? Another victory is in the crosshairs," she boasted playfully, turning her hand into a fake gun.

They both gathered their jackets off the rack and Noah headed back to drop some cash on the table to wipe out the bill. Jesse waited for him while he tied his shoes. They left the room stronger than they entered it, which was a little surprising to Jesse, but in a nice way.

They passed by the older ladies and then the sushi chef as a little blush found the cheeks of their faces. He narrowed his eyes at them (or maybe he didn't, they may have just naturally been that way), "Thank you! You come back again, yes?" he inquired with an unnecessary volume that would suit a jackhammer operator.

"Oh, definitely, sir, it was amazing!" Jesse replied, while Noah rubbed his abdomen in circles and smiled satisfyingly.

Once they exited the restaurant, one of the two elderly ladies looked at the chef and giggled. "Kids, they're just fucking crazy, aren't they? Breaking up one minute and back together the next. Ah, those were the days, weren't they?" she joked, visibly amused by the micro squabble.

The chef laughed at the remarks whole-heartedly. "Ha-ha-ha-ha-ha, oh, you very funny lady."

HALLOWEEN NIGHT

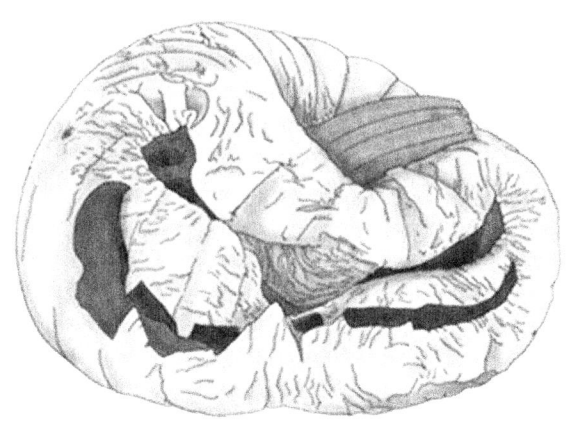

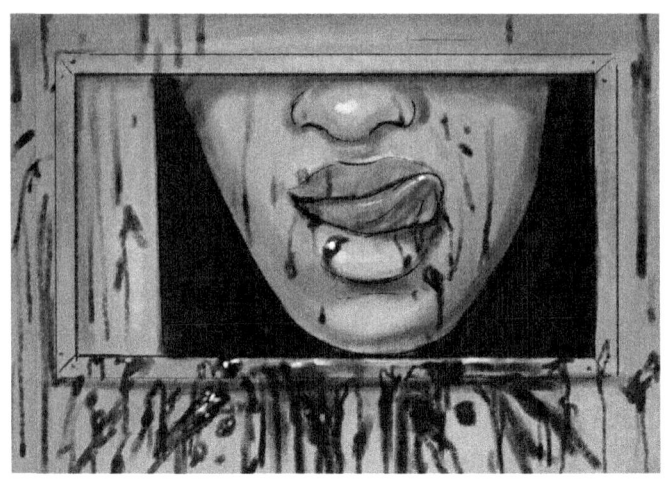

THE WICKED WAGER

Hershel walked over to Lawrence in the break room while he sat at a rectangular table devouring a PayDay bar. "You actually eat those?" Hershel questioned, put off by the sight.

"Yeah, I love peanuts, it's not uncommon," Lawrence confirmed.

"It's disgusting really."

"Listen, it's Halloween and we're the last two in the place for the night. We're stuck with each other, would you just let me enjoy my fuckin' candy in peace?"

"It's just a strange candy to enjoy is all I'm saying. I'm not even sure you're actually enjoying it, maybe you just think you are. I'm staring over at a minimum of a dozen or more superior selections in that machine."

"Tons of people love PayDay bars, Hershel… TONS. They wouldn't be in every single vending machine if they weren't popular."

"We got a real weird guy that takes care of the machines here, if you've seen him, you'd agree it's more than debatable if he's stocking the most popular products."

"Bullshit."

"Oh, it's bullshit? I got news for you, smart guy, people fuckin' hate those. How much you wanna bet it's not in the top ten best-selling candy bars? If you're so sure then just bet me."

"Well, what would the bet be?"

"If I'm wrong… I'll change Edmon's diaper the next three times when you're scheduled to. BUT if I win… you gotta change it tonight. That's how sure I am, I'll give you three to one odds." Hershel dangled the proposition over him carefully.

"Okay! Okay! Fine, you're on," Lawrence yelled, shaking Hershel's hand firmly.

"Well, go ahead, pull it up."

Lawrence picked up his phone from the table in front of him and Googled it. "Okay, here it is, the most recent stats. Number ten's a Hershey bar."

"Wow, I wouldn't have thought it would be that low…" Hershel replied.

"I know, that one almost sounds like your name. Number nine is… Oh, Henry bar? Really? Jesus that's a sleeper."

"They are good though. I don't eat 'em often but every once in a while, it's a nice change of pace," Hershel recalled fondly.

Number eight M&M's, number seven Baby Ruth, you see a lot of them got peanuts on the list so far, it's gotta be on here."

"We'll see, just keep going."

"Three Musketeers, Butterfinger, Milky Way."

"Ha! See! There's NO FUCKIN' WAY it's more popular than a Milky Way, this bet is over!"

"Kit-Kat… Reese's…"

"Go on…" Hershel nudged.

"Snickers…"

"Ah-ha-ha-ha! I knew it! Nobody eats that fuckin' bullshit! Just your dumb ass!"

"Damn it! How can it be?"

"I don't know, but on a side note, do you think Kit-Kat is a good name for a pet feline? It just doesn't sound like the name of a candy to me."

"Ughhhhhhh. I can't believe this shit."

"Good thing you ate BEFORE the bet, I don't think you'll have much of an appetite after your next activity. On the plus side, I already gave him the sedative for you. He should be sleeping in his chair, waiting politely."

"I can't believe I have to change that mutant's diaper on Halloween, what luck," Lawrence belly-ached.

"You already made it through your first week and you've only had the privilege of changing him once. It's time for round two. Don't worry though, you'll be fine, I just checked on him, he's out like a light."

Lawrence groaned while lifting himself from his seat and puttered out of the break room. The first time he'd changed him there were no issues, the sedatives they put in his mush knocked him out cold. It was just a particularly gross task. Even while Edmon slept, he made the disturbing wheezing noise that caused the loose flesh on his jaw to flutter.

Hershel pressed the red button fixed to the wall that unlocked his cell as Lawrence prepared himself for the nauseating event. He slapped on a pair of black disposable gloves before entering with the fresh diaper and a bin with a black garbage bag lining the inside.

Edmon sat faced away from him, angled toward the wall he loved to stare at. The inpatient chairs for an inhabitant that presented Edmon's level of danger were uniquely manufactured in such a way that suited it specifically for the intimate duty. The orderlies could reach around his hips through vacant lower areas of the skeleton seat and unfasten the sides, then clean and slide it out from underneath.

He set the bin just below his rear and started to unfasten it. But as the diaper came off of Edmon, he suddenly stood up… Lawrence rose quickly like his life depended on it, and turned around to see the cold filthy metal door of the cell slamming shut and locking.

Hershel's contentment could be seen through the door's opening, his buttery teeth on display for them both. Lawrence's face distorted as he turned around to witness Edmon's empty stare drilling through him. He began to shiver uncontrollably, still holding the soiled underwear and backing toward the closed door. The more disturbing facts of the story Hershel had outlined for him coming to life in the back of his psyche.

"What the fuck are you doing! Are you crazy? This isn't funny, Hershel, open it up! Open the fucking door now!" he pleaded with him.

"I'm afraid I can't do that. I wish I could, you're not a bad guy, Lawrence, but this is how it has to be." His evil smirk radiated in a way it hadn't in a long time.

Lawrence turned back to him and away from Edmon for a moment to further beg. "I'm sorry! Whatever I did, I'm sorry!" The sound of fabric ripping came next as Edmon tore through his strait-jacket in a way that seemed just a little too easy. It was almost like someone had previously loosened all of the restraints for him…

His massive hand clamped forcefully around Lawrence's skull, paralyzing his speech as he twisted him back so he was once again facing him. A muddle of horrific noises drained out from him as Edmon's other giant mitt enveloped both of Lawrence's quaking hands, which were still holding his nearly overflowing adult diaper.

The squirm-worthy sound of cracking bones resounded throughout the cell like an elephant stepping on a bundle of dry twigs. There was still too much pressure on Lawrence's temples for him to react, suffocating any potential for basic bodily functions as he continued to shake. He ripped the diaper filled with his feces from Lawrence's tremoring clutches and as he pulled it away, he left a trail of snapped fingers pointing in every imaginable direction. The digits looked like they were trying to run away from each other.

Running away was all Lawrence could think about when the feces hit his face and the diaper curled around it. The muddy thick shit would be his final meal as Edmon's mammoth closed fist launched through his face and then into the cell door behind him. His head couldn't have survived even a quarter of the blow's magnitude, let alone the full-bore shot. It erupted like a watermelon under Gallagher's sledgehammer, but the fillings were darker than a watermelon, especially being that they were infused into his excrement.

A wave of fluid, shit, and gore shot through the cell opening, landing across Hershel's smile. It dowsed the inside of his mouth and altered the color of his already imperfect teeth. Hershel swallowed the cocktail of horror like a thirsty dog as Lawrence's lifeless body thudded on the hard floor, his fleshy command center now forever closed.

"I told you, Lawrence! There's a lot of different flavors of shit to taste here!" he screamed at his still twitching corpse, releasing a maniacal laugh.

"Edmon," he whispered, straightening up. "I know what you want, you wanna see your momma, right? Well, guess what? Tonight's your lucky night," he explained, removing a small black and white aged photo from his top pocket.

He wiped some of the remaining bodily splatter off his face with his hand and licked his skin clean. He angled the faded photo through the door slot and dangled it like a carrot. Hershel offered the temptation to the hulking madman like he was the devil himself.

"I know you remember your mother, Edmon. I know you miss her. So, I'm gonna let you go out tonight and find her. Don't let anyone stop you. Don't let anyone get in your way. There's gonna be a lot of people that don't want you to find her. Bad, evil people. I think you know what to do with them though," he explained, speaking clearly and candidly. Hershel felt a sort of enthusiasm filling his insides that he never knew existed.

"How does that sound to you?"

Edmon gawked back at him, void of all response and expression. All he did was continue to breathe, inhaling in the only lone repugnant manner he knew. His output was the same as ever, but inside, he felt tremors. Inside, he felt rage. Inside, he felt hatred. He felt it for those who had separated him from his lone love and only advocate. A reflective, inky speck in his eye twinkled as he continued to stare at the decaying photo of his mother.

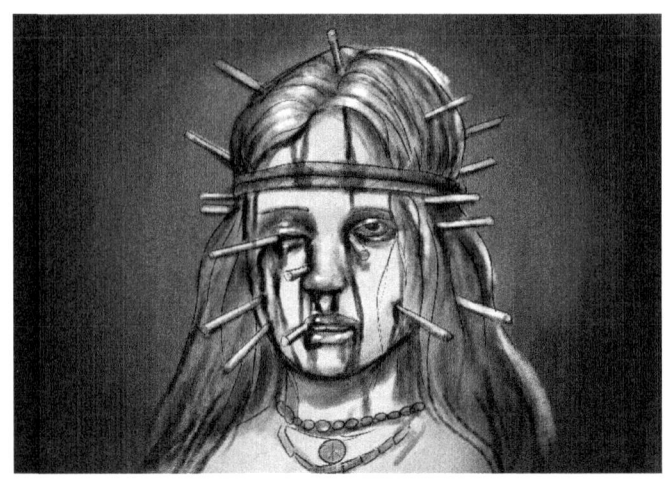

NO SANITY
NO SERVICE

The cluster of bells hanging from the door of the Tokyo Express rung a handful of times as Edmon stepped inside from out of the pitch-black darkness. His severely split strait-jacket was still showered with Lawrence's emissions and his own secretions. He'd slipped on a pair of the inpatient standard psychiatric pants and some ragged boots he'd acquired in the locker room. He appeared a distant separation from stability having failed to clean the sizable splattering of crimson and feces off his backside.

He was either the most disturbing real-life mess anyone would encounter in their lifetime, or an epic Halloween costume. Considering the proximity of the restaurant to the Ladd Institute, the chef chose not to believe the latter. The stench of funk and filth that was leaping off of Edmon was probably the tiebreaker. Even if it was a costume, it was bad for business—a real profit killer. No one was going to be able to swallow a bit of their meal with his rancid scent stirring about the dining room.

The skinny Japanese man slammed the meat cleaver down into the wooden board with the raw duck atop it. "Hey! I very sorry, we close now," he explained, crossing his arms behind the glass fish-meat case. "Please, you leave now."

Edmon did no such thing, not because he wanted to deliberately defy him but because he couldn't truly comprehend him. There was a likely chance it wouldn't have mattered anyway… he wasn't exactly in the mood to follow directions, considering that's all he'd ever done during his time on Earth.

There was only a tightknit group of patrons dining inside the restaurant at the time of his arrival. A threesome of stoned hippie chicks sat shoeless and Indian-style in the smaller room. The trio had just started sipping on their miso soup. They watched intently; all a tad unnerved after the ghastly-looking deranged lunatic had entered.

The cannabis they'd smoked and bag of gummies they'd been chewing on for the last few hours only served to further fester their paranoia. The sugary trip treats had just started to kick-in—what timing! Why was he here? Was it a joke? The questions jogging through their minds, which regardless of the correct answer, still left them lingering helplessly in a bizarre scenario. They needed to know if it was terrifying in a pay-to-enter haunted house kind of way, or a more reality-based horror. They listened to the flapping of his flesh from the destroyed portion of his face as their unease erected to a climax.

Edmon pointed at the glass containing the fish, his nasty dripping fingers smearing their vile coating all over the case. He tapped at it mindlessly as the peanut-colored concoction further blurred the visibility.

"I said out! Out!" the chef screamed, stepping around the case and positioning himself as if to square up with him. The guy had some balls, massive stones, in most cases, his aggression would've helped ward off an intruder or surly customer. Edmon had zero reaction to the chef stepping up initially, but when his reflexes were tested, the response was swift and unmerciful.

The chef laid a round-house kick up toward Edmon's head but it had no chance of reaching the target. It was stunted before it was ever a threat. Edmon's overgrown hand easily encased his foot, crushing and compressing it until it was just a leaking ball of bone, skin, and wetness. The ruby bones had splintered appallingly, piercing through his lightweight shoes. He fell to the ground, screaming in agony, slowly dragging himself back behind the main counter.

While shock set in on the chef, Edmon smashed the glass case in front of him and palmed a big glob that was a mixture of raw tuna and salmon. He mashed it up and inserted the soft-textured wad into his dangling, wrinkled feeding hole. Saliva raining out and the damp chunks of mush he was unable to swallow hit the floor below him.

He turned his attention to the three hippie girls as they headed for the door. He reached through the shattered glass and removed the massive cleaver from the cutting board.

As the frightened teens tried to single file their way out, Edmon took aim with the cleaver. Launching a Rodger Clements caliber fastball that sent the blade cycloning with an unforgiving projection. It landed smack in the center of the first girl's face, peeling down to the midway point of her brain. She fell, barreling backwards into her fellow meditating vegetarians, knocking them down like bowling pins.

He placed his Shaq-sized foot onto the flimsy chest of the girl who'd been the recipient of the cleaver. His dead weight pressed into her sternum, blaring out a sickening crunch and collapsing it inward. He pulled the handle and removed the stained steel, raising it once again. One of the two grounded girls started to gain her footing, so he sent it her way next. It landed deep in her shoulder and halfway through the wooden wall, pinning her to it.

She screamed like a maniac while bound to the boards in front of her. Her head was twisted sideways, leaving her to watch her only remaining friend as Edmon bent over and grabbed her by the hair. He dragged her back over to the small table that the evening had started off so enjoyably at. He grabbed a chopstick off the table in front of him, which looked more like a toothpick when surrounded by his hand.

He jammed it into her earhole and pressed his finger on the butt of it, making sure it went as deep as possible. She quivered and cried a short time before the second one came. She got a hand up but that did little to cushion the blow. He both impaled her hand and penetrated her forehead with the second stick. He ripped it back out and her bloody hand fell limp before he drove it right back in again. The part of the brain it pierced must have had something to do with communication because her vocal wailings cut out immediately.

He continued to put chopsticks through all the different angles of her head. It got easier as he progressed, she was seeing the light. By the end, atop the girl's shoulders looked closer to a game of Ker-Plunk than a human skull. A pinhead himself, Edmon had unknowingly created the wooden version of Clive Barker's legendary horror icon.

Edmon turned his attention back to the screaming girl restrained to the wall by the meat cleaver. He thrust a trio of his bulbous, sausage-like fingers around her jaw. A talon-like death-grip saw his index and middle fingers hook in between her molars while his thumb clamped firmly below her chin. Her tongue flailed about in many directions like a child running on the 4th with a sparkler. His muscle pulsated before he yanked backward, detaching the lower jaw entirely and tossing it behind him into a small koi pond. The underfed fish began to swirl about excitedly biting at the raw meat like savages, creating a restaurant role reversal.

Edmon followed up punching the exposed throat area he'd just created; the disgusting crunch caused the girl to shut down and slouch. She still remained standing even in death due to the massive steel blade pinning her to the wall. The weight of her body caused the edge of the steel to slice in deeper and exude a reservoir of red that one could have showered in.

Edmon shifted his attention back over to the chef. He could still hear a faint sobbing trickling out from the plastic streaming flaps that separated the kitchen from the dining room.

He laid holding his leg on the checkered tile floor when Edmon stepped inside. The chef glared up at him and spat while cursing in his native tongue. Edmon grabbed him by the neck and arched his back over the sink so his head was still facing him. The chef seemed like he might pass out from the suffering he was overcome with, eyes flickering in his head like the power kept switching on and off.

Edmon reached for a large pan of oil that remained on the stove beside them. He gazed down into the still sizzling and popping overused fluid, drawing the wok closer to the chef. He sloppily dumped the fine stream into his mouth, much of which seemed to run down him before it started making his face smoke and blister. Layer upon layer was burned through, the lighter skin had transitioned to a raw and painful red. He gagged and choked as Edmon continued pouring the rest of the lava-like lubricant.

Most of the flesh had been burned off from his mouth when Edmon reached for the second pan. The chef had ceased any movement—defenses were down and his breathing was faint. These factors made it easier for him to pour the entire additional pan down his esophagus with almost no spillage. On the second run, it scorched far down into his throat, eventually burning a gaping hole into the back of it. The oil that leaked from the freshly singed opening drizzled out slothfully into the sink below him. Edmon lifted the chef's lifeless body and tossed it on top of the lit grill before exiting. He left the kitchen to the stomach-churning sound of human skin searing behind him.

When Edmon was finally finished with the Tokyo Express, the interior looked like almost every inch had been decorated with the most unsettling Halloween decor of all time. As Hershel looked on, he knew that the mayhem he'd watched unfold was just a sample of things to come. He hadn't even seen him get to the young ones yet. He couldn't let it stop there…

He entered the restaurant and quickly flipped the open sign over to closed and dropped all of the blinds down. They'd been lucky that no one had seen the carnage unfolding inside, the area was dead, even before Edmon had shown up.

He marveled at the chaos Edmon had released up close, moving toward the far back of the restaurant before flipping all the lights off. He could smell a peculiar odor inside the eatery, something he wasn't familiar with. The sizzle of the grill drew him back toward the kitchen to investigate. It would be a miracle if anyone walked away from this massacre.

When he entered the kitchen, he zeroed in on the chef's corpse. It was motionless—bubbly and burned. It was a fire hazard; he didn't want police or firefighters getting a hint or showing up to put an end to Edmon's mayhem so early. Alertly, he dragged the body from the grill and turned off the heat. Crisis averted, Bedlam was still on the loose.

Suddenly, he heard a noise that sounded like someone coughing from down the hallway. He removed a revolver from the inside of his coat and inched closer until he came upon the men's room door. He opened it cautiously, noticing a pair of feet under the center stall.

Hershel quietly switched his position to the stall on the far left of the restroom which was right beside the sinks. When the stall's occupant exited, that would draw him right toward him, a slug would be the last thing he ever saw. But that wasn't the case, when the toilet flushed, a man wearing a cook's outfit exited the stall and failed to wash his hands as the sign on the wall demanded: "NOTICE: ALL EMPLOYEES <u>MUST</u> WASH HANDS BEFORE RETURNING TO WORK."

The son of a bitch ignored it, Hershel thought, rage beginning to swell. The man's ear buds were inserted firmly; he was oblivious to everything going on. Hershel rushed out of the bathroom, aiming the gun at him before he started screaming.

"Hey, you! Turn your ass around now!"

The man had no reaction and continued walking. Hershel cranked up the volume further, firing a shot into the air. The middle-aged man turned around hurriedly, frightened by the loud pop.

"You handling people's food in here! Why didn't you wash?"

"Please, I sorry! There no soap," he lied.

"You coulda still rinsed 'em off, why ain't you at least rinse it? I've eaten here before! Now I gotta think about your nasty ass makin' my meal. It's disgusting, it's… unacceptable."

"I very sorry, I go back and wash everything now, okay?" the man pleaded.

"That ain't gonna work, partna. People like you never change."

"I change! Never again, sir! Never again!"

"You'll always just be a filthy fuckin' slob."

Hershel pulled the trigger until it clicked, unleashing a hail of gunfire that peppered the cook from head to toe. The numerous wounds left cardinal colors spewing out of his carcass as he dropped to his knees and tumbled over sideways. He tried to make a final statement, maybe a deathbed confession, but history would not be able to catalogue it. All that Hershel could make out were a few sad cries and gurgles.

SCARY BASTARD

Timmy and his sister, Ann, sat fidgeting in the back of the wagon as the full moon's glow trickled in through the windows. Timmy's Scarecrow outfit was a great compliment to his sister's Dorothy outfit. His dad was the Lion, and of course, that would make his mom the Wicked Witch of the West.

"Are we there yet?" Timmy barked, developing more impatience with each mile they drove.

"Damn it, Timmy, I told you we're almost there. Now STOP asking," Donald fired back at his son, finally fed up with the constant nagging.

"Mommy, it's not gonna be too scary, is it?" Ann inquired in a cowardly tone that most five-year-olds would find themselves exercising at one point or another.

"No, honey, just remember, it's all make-believe. They are all just dressed up like us, having fun for

Halloween. Everyone wants to scare each other, but really, there isn't anything to be scared of," Ruth reassured her.

"Really?"

"Really. Have I ever lied to you before, sweetie?" Ann shook her head. "Plus, me and Daddy would never let anything happen to you, okay, baby?"

Ann grinned, brandishing her tiny teeth and looking up at her mother. The explanation comforted her.

"Here we are!" Donald bellowed out while pulling onto the dirt road. It was easy for them to find parking since there were only a handful of cars in the gravel lot. "Aren't you glad we came early? No one is even here yet," Donald asked, looking over to Ruth.

"You were right. Great call, honey," she concurred, kissing him on the lips before leaving the car.

Donald let his I-told-you-so smirk hang on his face. To him, there was never a doubt about it.

They all walked up to the slender vampire standing at the head of the corn maze, thumbing at his phone. "Did Dracula do a lot of texting?"

The carefree boyish vampire looked up at him, "I'm Nosferatu, sir, thank you. How many?" he remarked without really answering the question.

"C'mon, man, you're killing the atmosphere and we haven't even got in yet," Donald quipped.

"Donald, just forget it. Two children and two adults please," Ruth responded, shifting gears from her husband's sharp critiques.

"Here you are, that will be sixty-five dollars please," the vampire replied while handing over their tickets.

"Sixty-five dollars! American dollars you mean? Are you out of your mind? Now I know why you people don't put the prices on your site! This is just a field, man, are you kidding?"

"Sir, I'm going to have to ask you to please calm down and not yell."

Ruth handed the money over to the vampire quickly after the brief tantrum, knowing they weren't turning around purely based on a stiff price. They'd never hear the end of it from the kids and that alone was worth the price of admission.

Donald looked him in the eye, squinting before moving on. "I get it now."

"Get what, sir?" he asked in a condescending tone that indicated he had zero interest in Donald's answer.

"Your costume. You guys really are just a bunch of fuckin' bloodsuckers, aren't you?" he jabbed before moving past him.

"Donald!" Ruth exclaimed, smacking him in the chest before dragging him away from the shell-shocked teen. "That type of language in front of the kids?" she whispered to him. "We don't want Timmy learning any other words, remember!"

"Right, I'm sorry, honey. It's just, this place is a fuc— I mean freakin' racket. This is completely outside the reigns of reason."

"I agree, but the kids really want to see it, so let's not let the price stop us from having a good time, okay?"

"That's right, baby, we're good parents. You're right. This is why I married you. That and you have a really nice as—" Ruth cut off his crude remark with an affectionate kiss. Holding it for long enough to calm him down before they caught up to the kids.

"Hey, Timmy, buddy, slow down. We wanna go through this together, okay?"

The children came to a halt, waiting for their

parents before moving any further. They collectively took some slow steps, taking in the creepy atmosphere that the dimly lit cornfield had to offer. It was really dark but the possible trail paths were lit at the base by bundles of orange lights.

As they came to the first fork in the path, Donald looked down at Timmy for guidance. "Okay, buddy, what's it gonna be? We'll let you pick the first one. Left or right?"

"Left!" Timmy screamed, racing down the path like a bat out of hell. They could still see him a bit further up as he neared another corner, but instead of blazing the trail further, he stopped dead in his tracks.

"Da-Dad! Mom!"

The rest of the family all hustled up toward him quickly, anxious to see the first display that seemed to have Timmy so startled. Donald figured that it must have been pretty cool because his boy was not known to rattle easily.

As they got closer, the picture came into focus—a man dressed as a clown sat atop a few bales of hay, his head completely missing and a mushy pile of crushed humanity strewn over his lap. Donald stood by the man viewing the blood still oozing down from his jumbled neck area.

"How do they make it look so real? When you look close, it's even bleeding, babe."

"I thought this maze was appropriate for children?" Ruth whispered back to him.

"It said it was, I mean, that idiot out front even sold us passes for the kids. This fuckin' place is something else," Donald moaned, now even more irate than when he'd entered.

"Fuckin' place!" Timmy yelled.

"Timmy! Hey! Watch the language, mister!" Ruth reprimanded.

"Yeah, bud, you can't say that. It's an adult word." Donald reminded him.

"Damn it, Donald! This is exactly what I was talking about," Ruth raged.

Ann started to hear a strange wheezing noise from behind her while the family rambled on arguing with each other. The meat flapping as oxygen was sucked in, the struggle to exist. She turned around only to be faced with a primal blood-soaked figure that towered overhead. Edmon's ghoulish representation was far scarier than anything she'd ever laid eyes on before.

"Moooooooom. Daaaaaaaad," Ann drawled out in a way that conveyed exactly how disturbed she was by what she was seeing and hearing. "Why's he breathing like that?"

Donald turned around and gasped, taken aback momentarily by his stature and the evil manifested over his flesh. "Whoa! Jeeze! You scared us there for a second. You're, ha, you're one scary bastard now, aren't you?" Edmon remained motionless, watching them closely.

"Daddy, tell him to stop making that noise, it's scaaaaary…" Ann requested sheepishly while she backed away from him. It was apparent tears would be on the way if the noise didn't stop. She retreated behind her parents as Ruth and Donald stood side by side still amazed by his presence.

"Say friend, you're doing a heck of a job out here. This place really is terrifying but my little girl… she, well, we thought this was a family-friendly kind of place. It might be a little intense for her. Do you think you could just stop the noise for a minute so she knows it's fake?"

Edmon took a step closer to them, his chest now right up to their noses, his fetid scent pushing outward. A second later, his breathing stopped.

Donald looked up at him trying to suppress his disgust for what he was inhaling, while Ruth held her nose. "Boy, you guys really take this stuff seriously. How long did you go without bathing leading up to this?" he chuckled awkwardly.

Edmon still gave no reply as Donald turned back to his daughter who was now yards away from them in the outskirts of the maze.

"Baby, he's just playing a monster. He stopped making the noise, you can come back over here now, okay?" Ann was registering what he was saying but still remained hesitant, examining his deformed frame as she stood speechless and shaking.

"It's fine, baby, he's not gonna do anythi—"

Donald's final words were cut short by the collision of his skull with his wife's. The old adage two heads are better than one had come to life, and the soulmates quickly learned there was no literal truth to the saying. Edmon's mammoth hands clapped together, sending shards of cranium bone, blood, and sopping meat erupting into the air. Their bodies hit the dirt static as the piñata load of bloodshed showered all over Timmy. His tiny lungs revved up, radiating horror as Edmon rapidly got his hands around him.

With Edmon's back turned, Ann melted into the thick cornstalks and watched Timmy while staying hidden in a darkened patch of field. While tears streamed for her parents, her dread kept her in check. Somehow, she was able to find the strength to maintain a suffocating silence. Ann was still hopeful that her brother might find a method of escape. She prayed to God that he'd give him the means to slip away. She wanted to call out to him and tell him to run but feared the next word she spoke could potentially be her last.

She continued praying in her head, screaming out telepathically, but it didn't make a difference. Her nervous prayer was abruptly snuffed out when Edmon removed a scarecrow puppet from the sharpened stick it had been impaled upon. He set it up at a slightly diagonal angle.

Edmon stared expressionlessly at the whittled wood projecting upward, running his meaty finger over the tip that stood about his height. He lifted up Timmy's squirming body and set him down swiftly. As the moonlight embraced them, the sharpened spike drove up into his ass, splintering into his rectal tissue. He pulled him up and down, violently sodomizing the boy and further opening the blood-filled, shitty gape that had permanently stretched his innocent asshole.

The hot red fluid filled Timmy's suit as Edmon now stopped fluctuating the boy and applied more pressure. As he worked him further down the oak shaft, the jagged wood continued its travel up through his stomach and bowels. He'd stopped screaming as a mixture of his feces, blood, and intestines made their way out of his mouth. The forced regurgitation of his innards left him shaking and silent. Timmy struggled to free himself as he finally lost control of his bodily functions.

Edmon stood stationary as if admiring his handy work. He looked up at the yellow moon in the background and then back to the boy. He grabbed hold of the rust-laced pitchfork wedged inside one of the hay bales in the area before refocusing on him.

Ann watched silently as the life drained out of her brother. She did everything she could to avoid making the slightest noise while Edmon drove the weathered tool through him until it was butted up directly against the boy's neck. Red rained down over the front of his outfit as Ann bit down hard on her fist. Timmy had become his costume.

CEMETARY STRAIN

Jesse and Noah sat together near an old crypt while he finished twisting the joint ends shut. Her Species costume had come to life, it was by far the best thing she'd ever produced. She only wished there was a mirror around them the whole night to keep admiring it. After time faded, the memories wouldn't do it justice. They'd better be sure to take a few videos too.

Noah, on the other hand, looked like he just got out of work—his costume was thoughtless and boring. Asylum worker was more dated than a calendar and excruciatingly unoriginal. The kind of costume that was overlooked at conception, it had never been intriguing. Jesse spruced it up as best she could with splats of her homemade fake blood recipe. At least that added a little color. It always amazed her how you could cover just about anything under the moonlight in blood and it would look fucking stellar.

Noah lit up the joint and took a deep drag, "You know, we could've just drove. They let me borrow the Fiat again."

"Who wants to drive on Halloween? Don't you like walking down the streets and seeing the freaks and monsters all around you? And there's nowhere I'd rather be than this graveyard. It feels so right being at a place like this tonight. Don't you think?"

"Yeah, it's lovely…" he replied, taking an additional hit while Jesse watched the orange tip flare.

"We're not gonna be young forever. Soon, this day will be more for our kids than us."

Noah let out a deep cough, seemingly caught off guard, "Kids? Did I miss something? When did we plan on having kids?"

"Ha, I meant any *potential* kids we might have, you know… after we're done with college and living our dreams and shit. Everyone always thinks it's going to last forever but I'm betting it'll be over before we know it. At least that's what every miserable parent I bump into repeats."

"Jesus, you really are an old soul. Let's not get too depressed though, we're trying to have ourselves a good night now, aren't we?" Noah reminded her, finally passing over the joint.

She took another deep drag and held it for about seven seconds, responding while exhaling. "Right on."

"Well, it's puff, puff, pass, isn't it? C'mon, you know the rules, no getting more stoned than me!" he joked, holding his hand out.

"What is this stuff anyway?"

"Well, they're calling it the Cemetery Strain. Muuuuhahahahha." His maniacal voice was ridiculous.

"No, seriously, what is it? Tastes almost, moldy…"

"I'm not joking, that's what they call it."

"What? Do they call it that because it tastes like something died?"

"No, it's actually a little more serious than that. I guess the kid that created the strain took in a little too much of it. He accidentally knocked over his ashtray while he was passed out… and whoosh! His whole house went up in smoke."

"You're lying!" Jesse yelled, punching him in the arm with a hard shot.

"Ouch! Relax, Rhonda! I'm for real. I heard aside from the few pounds that he sold prior to the fire, everything went up in smoke that night. A few weeks later, the city started canning tons of the firefighters left and right. All their piss tests were coming up sour. Turns out that the investigators reviewed the house and uncovered the problem. All the firefighters battling the blaze were breathing in copious amounts of the most potent ganja. It was all of the fuckin' smoke from his stash and grow farm that got them higher than Hendrix."

"That's so insane. You really have an unbelievable excess of useless but highly entertaining information."

"Thank you? I think for the most part it's all just marketing, people make up crazy-ass names for things that sound fun, they usually have nothing to do with the product. I mean, do you wanna just smoke some weed? Or do you wanna smoke the blueberry purple-coaster crush?"

"Same as a happy-meal, they're not really selling food in that name, more just happiness, I guess," Jesse agreed.

"Damn right they are. The concept still somehow gets me hungry though, either that or all the weed we're always smoking…"

"Well, what do you say we get to the party then?"

"Definitely, just a second here."

Noah bent down and picked up the 40oz of King Cobra from beside the gravestone and started chugging the remaining third of the bottle until it had all disappeared. He tossed the empty carelessly in front of him and it landed beside a relatively new stone. He turned toward it and unzipped himself.

"Noah, what the hell are you doing! Don't you have any respect?" Jesse screamed out in anger.

"Oh, c'mon, Jess. Do you really think…" he paused, focusing for a moment on reading the name of the headstone, "that Emily Black cares? She's in heaven or something, not here anymore…" he said, beginning to slur his words.

When Noah finished, he turned around to find Jesse had left him behind. She was storming back toward the gates less than amused by Noah's dickhead antics.

"Hey, Jess, wait up! I was just messing around!" he yelled, zipping his fly while still trying to play catch-up.

THIS PLACE IS A ZOO

The Jack-O'-Lantern Spectacular was one of the most highly anticipated and entertaining activities of the year at Rodger Williams Park & Zoo. Picture hundreds and hundreds of highly detailed pumpkins carved out to perfection with their orangey interiors illuminated. They had everyone from Prince to Ren & Stimpy, to George W. Bush, to Gremlins accounted for.

It was the perfect balance of celebrity intertwined with scary. It embodied all of the staple slashers of the horror genre, as well as the lesser-knowns. It was a mesmerizing stroll overrun with couples and families all wanting to be a part of the compelling Halloween aura and creepy festivities.

The path that people were led down was normally

the zoo trail. If you came at just the right time, you could see both the animals and nature mixed with the macabre and chilling ornamentation. The place was a favorite for locals leaving the parking lot always jammed to a bursting capacity. The Jack-O'-Lantern Spectacular was exactly that.

Every year after the last tour, all the park hands and zookeepers got together to throw a little bash and spoil the animals with some treats. Juan had been working at the zoo for just over three years, he knew how the celebrations went. This was like their Christmas party since the zoo didn't really operate during the brutal winter months.

They went all out, kind of a one-day hall pass to do or say anything and then see how the chips fell. Last year, they'd fallen the way Juan could have only dreamt. After a few dozen drinks, the group was inebriated beyond repair. At the time, he was relatively new and viewed as an intriguing commodity amongst his female counterparts.

Everyone was so fucked up that fucking was the only reasonable progression from there, and fuck they did. He'd sat down on the Ronald McDonald bench near the ostriches when the overly intoxicated Isabelle followed him out. She'd been chatting in a secret and mischievous manner with her girl, Evelyn, for the better part of the evening. It seemed like a wonderful drunken conspiracy when Evelyn followed behind her just a few moments later.

The end result was an incredibly sloppy (but satisfying) threesome that transpired in the nippy chill of the frigid autumn air. They used the ridiculous park bench while the birds watched on. It was actually a foursome if you counted the life-size plastic Ronald

McDonald figure fused to the bench surface beside them. He couldn't really do much, but he got a lot of cheap rubs in.

Isabelle and Evelyn were there again but they seemed to really take a liking to the new guy, Mark. It might not just fall into place like last Halloween, he might need to do a bit of strategizing this round. Mark was alone with them now, so Juan knew he needed to lock up quickly and get back before they found a new flavor of the year. They usually left the pumpkins lit while they partied, so the path to the front glowed eerily while he was en route.

Once he reached the gates, he snapped the bulky Master lock over the big chain and snapped it shut. "Now it's time to get back to the bitches," he whispered, looking down at his junk. "Right?" he asked, posing the question to his penis like he was expecting it to say something back.

The conversation he was having with himself was broken up by a shriek coming from the chimpanzee exhibit. They began pounding and rattling the steel fencing violently. It wasn't a completely uncommon occurrence but he still thought he should check on them. As he got closer to the bellows of the chimps, he saw a massive ominous figure looming in the shadows. The figure sat just outside of the glow of the jack-o'-lanterns. He assumed that they might have a straggler from the last run and inched a little closer to him.

The chimps were going bananas now, absolutely losing their minds. Overcome with fury, it was easy to understand that they hated the presence. Their frothing mouths jabbered madness and their eyes filled with fury while their crooked fingers curled around the metal fencing.

"Hey, chief, the last walkthrough ended about thirty minutes ago. Anyone else with you?" he asked the figure, anticipating a response. After another few beats of silence, he tried once more. "I'm going to have to take you to the gate, we can't have anyone in here after hours. We're closed."

Juan was a pretty stout kid and felt confident when it came to self-defense. A few years of boxing at the YMCA and having to trek through a rough South Providence hood regularly while growing up had galvanized his exterior. If the guy wanted to throw hands, he was happy to appease him. Hopefully, it didn't come to that but a fight here or there could get the blood flowing.

He began to hear something previously muddled by the outrage of the chimps—something odd. He couldn't quite place what it was at first until he noticed the shape's chest puffing in and out to the rhythm. It was a haggard, struggling breathing pattern like an old man wheezing. "Hey, dude, is everything okay? You having trouble breathing?"

He approached him as he finished his question but only once his eyes had finally adjusted to the dark, he could see the disturbing qualities of the odd character before him. He realized immediately that he'd made a mistake, a herculean, blood-soaked psychopath wasn't the one he was looking to throw with. The chimp's unruliness and hissing only intensified as Edmon grabbed Juan by the shirt and drove his gargantuan fist into his nose. As his target hit the ground, blood drained from his bent nose like a dozen periods. Edmon used both hands to elevate his stunned body above his head and toss him over the railing.

He accomplished the strenuous task with the ease

of reprimanding a child. Juan's body landed in the dirt near about four of them. They wasted no time in going to work on him. One of the animals restrained his arms while another bit down on his hand. When it pulled its mouth away, only his thumb and a chewed-up pinky had managed to remain intact. The chimp, tired of his horrified moans, quickly grabbed hold of his tongue and placed his clubbed foot on Juan's forehead. It pulled back mightily as its bicep bulged, the sound of the tough mouth muscle ripping through the autumn air could be heard. After some additional effort, the wet meat split entirely away from Juan's blood-filled orifice and the chimp began to chomp on the gamey, jumping muscle. It took some concentrated chewing but after a few seconds, it managed to swallow it.

Edmon kept watching quietly as they continued Juan's destruction. Somehow, he'd fended them off and made it back to his feet. He closed his mouth and tried to contain the massive amount of blood he was losing from where his tongue had been taken. He staggered, cheeks looking like a pufferfish and the red trickled down his chin.

Suddenly, another chimp came from behind him and punched him in the balls. The blow was so stiff that it forced him to blow the blood-load in his mouth and spit it all over his aggressor. This seemed to only further agitate as the chimp followed up with an additional nut-cracking assault that caused him to bend forward and fall to his knees.

Next, they shredded through his pants, leaving his lower area exposed. Although Juan's speech had been disabled, he still tried to beg them to stop with his eyes and inaudible murmurs. They did no such thing, instead, the mother seemed to be attracted by his pathetic sniveling actions.

She set a crushing hold upon both his wrinkly nuts with one hand and his limp cock in the other and pulled them in opposite directions. She dug her coarse fingers into the bottom of Juan's ballbag and used the sharpness of her nail tips to create an opening above his taint.

As the red oozed out, she stuck her fingers into his scrotum, enlarging the hole that she'd created. After a moment of fishing around, her digits got entangled in his vas deferens. She tugged violently on the flesh cords that had allowed his nuts to dangle for nearly twenty-four years. There was no going back now, his days of dangling were done.

She ripped out the entire ejaculatory duct along with all they fed into. As Juan looked on, paralyzed in pain, she made pulling off his penis look much easier than his nuts were. She didn't eat all of it herself, she gave part of his testicles to her babies. Her unhinged children then quickly gathered around her as they graciously devoured his sexual organs together.

Edmon watched one of the smaller ones pull at Juan's face, removing chunk after chunk of skin and flesh from him until hints of his facial bones started to uncover. He was either already dead or too in shock to offer a proper reaction.

The chimp screeched playfully and stretched the torn off globs of Juan's face over its own and tried to scare the other monkeys in its family. It almost seemed like they were playing their own little Halloween tricks on each other. They had become much calmer since abolishing Juan. Their hype dropped down to a simmer and they were suddenly so filled with joy that they were hardly making a peep about anything anymore.

MEANWHILE, BACK AT THE RONALD MCDONALD BENCH…

Juan's worst fears had come to life. Before he'd made it back, Mark had found his way to the sacred spot with both Isabelle and Evelyn by his side. There could be no annual repeat with his corpse rendered comatose and his cock in the belly of a baby chimp. But Isabelle and Evelyn weren't even privy to those details yet, and that's the kind of thing that can make a ghost sad.

The October air had made it a tit nipply out and the three of them had been working furiously to keep each other warm. The two girls both had their legs spread wide. Mark's face was buried between Isabelle's while Evelyn rubbed her clit and watched. It would have been her turn next but she was the only one with her eyes open—just her and Ronald.

Their panting and embellishment had been so loud that none of them were able to really notice the breathing and flapping of Edmon's face until it was already too late. Evelyn took off so quickly and fear-stricken that they didn't even notice until Edmon was already on top of them. He struck Isabelle in the windpipe, putting an end to the passionate moans she was expelling out so generously. Her thin neck had crumbled under his absurd power. The spine bone snapped sideways and forced her tan skin to rise upward like a tent. Her head had snapped backward and was limply hanging behind the back of the bench, swinging slowly back and forth.

When her legs dropped their full weight down on Mark's shoulders, he took his face out of her snatch for a moment and looked up. To him, it just looked like she was leaning really far back, and that image was the last thing he ever saw. Edmon's colossal hand forced the back of his head forward and using his abnormal power, he grinded Mark's face back and forth against her vaginal area. The sadistic friction of his suffocation was starting to wreck her lips and violently enlarge her opening.

Edmon used his other hand to pull Mark's lips back and used his crooked enamel to cut into her irritated pink entrance. The Neanderthal-level of aggressiveness Edmon displayed left a wake of messy chafing. After a few minutes, his brute force had torn right through the vaginal track and into her anus, merging them into one mammoth gaping hole. Mark choked on her fleshy wetness while Edmon held him in place. The machine-like pressure he applied caused areas of his skull to collapse as he tried to make him fit. Moments later, Isabelle's newly created smelly space had completely engulfed Mark's entire skull. His broken head was wholly submerged in her nether-region, so far that Isabelle's clit was now resting tiredly on the back of his shiny neck.

While Ronald looked on (happily, the only way his rigid design permitted), Mark's head vanished inside Isabelle's new hole and he wiggled about wildly like a fresh worm on a fisherman's hook. It didn't take long for him to stop moving, about the length Mark could've held his breath underwater. He died with the scent of skank bombarding his smell factory, suffocated by the very thing he cherished most in life; pussy.

Once Edmon felt his pulse lose its rhythm, he gazed down at the destroyed pair of perverts and then over to Ronald again. His psychotic glare pressed the plastic clown replica as if he was waiting for him to animate somehow and then put an end to him like the others. It took a few more moments of scrutiny before he finally broke the futile stare.

Evelyn was still completely naked when she made it to the front gates. She should've known Juan probably wouldn't be there still and that there was also a high probability that they'd be locked already. She screamed hysterically, once again agitating the chimps that were not too far away. No one was in earshot, but she was foolishly giving up her position to the maniac on the loose by belting out all of her terrors.

She piped down, realizing that would do her no favors and ran off down the trail. She bolted past the bears and the golden lion exhibits until she'd reached the World of Adaptations section. She stopped to rest and assess her surroundings just as she reached the Komodo dragons. She was out of breath when she noticed the dragon's becoming disturbed by her presence. They hissed at her loudly, they were more than worked up by her arrival.

She'd never seen them react that way, they were not commonly loud creatures by nature, yet they were almost ascending to a deafening pitch. As she turned her attention toward the reptiles, a hand wrapped around the back of her neck and lifted her off the ground. Edmon drove her down—backbone-first—onto the rocky concrete lip of the exhibit and listened to a group of vertebrae pop in sequence.

He dumped Evelyn's shocked body over the wall and she landed awkwardly with her left shoulder and neck being the first thing to hit the hard dirt. The fall by some miracle hadn't killed her, but the Komodos surely would. They pounced on the uncommon sight without hesitation, biting frantically at her maimed immobile frame. Each time the tiny razor teeth burrowed into her, she cried. She screamed without end as they picked her apart, ripping through her soft tissues without reservation.

Edmon related to the absence of mercy in the cold-blooded beasts as he watched them deconstruct her in ghoulish fashion. Her bare body rapidly progressed to a redder chewed-up form with each blink of his eye. If he could've smiled, he might have.

The one positive for Evelyn was that she could no longer feel the mauling that was occurring from the shoulders down, but the bites that stole chunks of her face were still extremely agonizing. She stared up at Edmon with the golden moon backlighting his chiseled hulking border, wondering why it all came to this. She was about to die and hadn't even gotten laid that night.

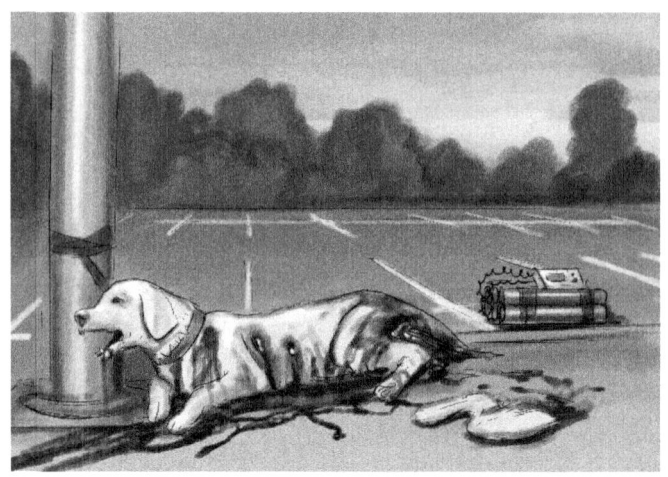

THE VOLATILE VIRGINS

Both Chaz and Winston had tired of an existence without pussy. There was nothing that a couple of boys their age thought about more. Neither had ever been capable or confident enough to land a girlfriend, but that part didn't bother them so much. They were cool just hanging out with each other. They didn't need the girls themselves around, just their warm wet pleasure sockets. At least that's how they understood it…

"Drink beers & beat up queers" was their slogan. A phrase they liked to say around people to let them know that they only did awesome stuff. Queers didn't necessarily have to be someone who was gay, they also used the term to describe anyone they felt was lame. Targeting and harassing people was about their favorite pastime, aside from kicking the shit out of them.

Additionally, some of their other hobbies included vandalizing historic areas, breaking into and destroying cars, playing Mortal Kombat, killing helpless animals, lighting shit on fire, and of course, the extensive researching and planning of mass murders…

Destruction, hatred, immaturity, idiocy, and involuntary celibacy were probably the words that best described them. Most were words that would've all felt complimentary to them though. They salivated over the idea of committing famous crimes the ilk of Dylan Klebold and Eric Harris.

They'd continued to discuss the concept on a fanatical basis, looking up to the pair like other teens would their favorite musician. They watched endless crime documentaries on the topic, all the archival footage they'd left behind, and both had carefully read Dave Cullen's book, Columbine, on multiple occasions.

The challenge of making it happen wasn't as difficult as it would have been for most teens in their shoes. Their unique niche lifestyles allowed them the opportunity for anarchy. A few detailed arrangements and they would find a way to get there. They would capture the infamy that other evil people had before them and live on for generations haunting parents, another morbid and chilling example of how ordinary teens spiral out of control.

Chaz's father was a doomsday prepper who had stocked an arsenal that looked like it was straight out of a fucking Schwarzenegger flick in the tool shed out back. An eclectic collection of killing devices, some of which were highly illegal. It wasn't just guns either, there was everything from swords to brass knuckles, to throwing knives, and ninja stars. A spree killer's wet dream. The best part was that the entire stash was merely restricted by a single snap-on lock. A pair of bolt cutters and they'd be inside that bitch in seconds.

Since Chaz had concocted a viable plan to acquire the weaponry, Winston was tasked with making the bomb. He'd spent the entirety of their sophomore year looking through various online manuscripts and the Anarchist's Cookbook (amongst other versions of the popular guide to troubles). He'd made a variety of duds initially, but so had the Columbine killers. In fact, the bomb they'd brought into the school was a big dud, which (sadly in their eyes) would end up seriously hampering their kill count. Looking back on the whole ordeal, it felt to them like the missed opportunity had cheapened the entire legacy.

It was up to Winston to ensure that their legacy didn't suffer a similar fate. He'd been working quite diligently to make that happen. Just a few weeks prior, he'd asked Chaz to meet him at The Bug Club. It was an old decrepit building out in the middle of nowhere.

The Bug Club was a highly popular bar back in the 70s. The seedy backdrop of the establishment was kind of a giant open secret. It was typically leveraged as a swinger couple hook-up spot. A place where a pair of sexually promiscuous married folks that wanted to spice things up again might link up with another like-minded duo over a few overpriced drinks. Eventually, the religious types in town got wind of it and boycotted them right out of business. The death of The Bug Club came in response to the morality issues exhaustively outlined by the obsessive evangelical populous… basically because people got tired of driving so fucking far for strange sex…

The Bug Club was dead. Dead to everyone except Chaz and Winston that is. It now served as the headquarters where they deliberated their deranged futures. The meeting grounds for the master plot was a quiet place where they could record themselves and their perverse process leading up to the massacre. Similar to how their idols did in a basement.

They also used the hidden concrete area behind it to test out their equipment. They would usually take turns firing an old Glock that Chaz had swiped from his father's stash and talking about the plan obsessively. There were so many pieces in the shed that he knew just swiping a single outdated gun wouldn't raise his fanatical father's suspicions. They'd practice their shooting and aim with the lone gun in preparation. If other weapons kept vanishing, that could risk the integrity of their operation. When shit went down, it would have to be a big bang kind of deal. They'd clean out the shed altogether, everything in one shot.

When Chaz arrived at The Bug Club, he found Winston firing the pistol out back already. Except, he quickly noticed that he wasn't aiming it at the malt liquor empties like they usually did. Instead, Chaz was treated to the site of Ringo, tied to an inactive telephone pole near the peripheries of the woods behind the building. Ringo was the family dog of a boy they had beef with. A beautiful border collie owned and beloved by a fellow classmate of theirs by the name of Charles Buckley.

As Chaz rested his eyes on the pup his hatred began to bubble inside. The gist of the animosity was they didn't like Charles for two reasons. The first being that he was black and the second being that he was popular with the girls. At a high-level, the only issue was that they were jealous racists. Of course, they didn't see it that way though. One day, they'd caught Charles by surprise en route home from football practice.

They'd monitored his patterns for a few weeks to understand his path. Over time, they observed that Charles usually took a shortcut home that shaved off about ten minutes from his hike. The area was desolate and secluded, perfect for what they were thinking… They saw him trailing down the ratty vacant catwalk before hitting the train tracks for about half a mile. It was an ideal spot for an ambush if there ever was one.

The normally private and serene path turned into anything but when Chaz hit Charles with a cattle prod from behind. They had a bag over his head before he could shake off the stun and get a look at their faces. They worked together and tied him to the train tracks, shocking him another half-dozen times with the prod for good measure.

The electrocution left his restrained body jerking, cries of pain and dismay emanated down the corroded tracks for miles. Spitting on him, kicking his ribs, and yelling insults wasn't enough. They wanted him dead. Sure, they might have killed him during the shooting or explosion they were planning at school, but that wasn't an absolute inevitability. Shit got crazy in those situations and they needed to know he was dead before them—anything else left a slice to chance still.

"We found you a ride home, nigger, so now you don't have to walk!" Chaz sneered, pointing down the railroad as if a train was approaching.

"Yeah, free of charge, Chuck Buck! You ain't gotta worry about the shortcut no more. Your black faggot ass is gonna be a pile of fuckin' pieces any minute now," Winston added.

Winston kicked him in the ribs even harder this time and they proceeded to pound from top to bottom unmercifully. After splitting his lips and leaving their lumps, they left him to die on the tracks. Beaten bloody with a bag on his head, there were few options for Charles. The trains ran about every four to five hours and most people didn't walk on the railway at all, so it was miraculous when Junkie Jim stumbled upon him.

Junkie Jim, or "JJ" as all the kids in the area called him, was a walking punchline. Mocked by the stable nucleus of society for his fiendish ways and the litter of track marks that speckled his arms. He was a forgotten, a fringe player, a beggar, a shitty and typically devious bum. A man who'd lost his ethics long ago when his mother overdosed on bad meth and left him in the cradle to rot. His distorted principles had shifted from the social regular to someone that only existed to put himself first.

His nastiness could be viewed from a distance. The oil stains on his trench coat were nearly as black as his soul. The only holiness about him lay in his clothing; he was ripped to shreds like homework that the dog got into. His stretching beard was filthy but did the small kindness of shielding his rotten teeth (of which he only had maybe a handful left) from anyone who came face to face with him.

He must have enjoyed the lonely solitude the area normally afforded him. Once he'd done his robbery or panhandled enough to acquire what he needed to get his fix, he'd shoot his dope and pass out near the edge of the woods. The railway was his favorite spot to needle up, a concept that Chaz and Winston had failed to anticipate.

On most days, Junkie Jim would have just sat there

and watched the body parts fly but something different was inside him that day. Maybe it was because Charles reminded him a little of the story he'd been told about himself. When he was left to die in the cradle after his mother's heart exploded, he was helpless. It took someone else to save him. It took a stranger's kindness to save him. It took a stranger's pity on his situation to pull him from the depths of desperation.

If it hadn't been for that sympathetic stranger, he wouldn't be able to run around like an animal shootin' dope all day. He could feel it, there was some weirdness brewing inside him that morning. He was about to do something that was so irregular, he even shocked himself a little too. He was about to do a good deed… but not just simply out of the kindness of his heart, and certainly not for free.

He told Charles he'd have to give him enough money for another dose if he wanted any help. He quickly redacted the initial proposal and instead asked for forty bucks, enough for TWO more doses. Charles could tell that the words were coming from someone else by the aged raspy tinge and just overall defeat in Junkie Jim's voice. He agreed to the selfish terms and was subsequently untied. Charles removed the money from his wallet and paid Junkie Jim as promised. The two of them never spoke of the incident again.

Chaz finally snapped back out of his trip down memory lane grinding his teeth in displeasure. While the attempted murder of Charles Buckley hadn't quite gone as planned, they were sure that they'd have better luck next time. They'd be stopping at his classroom first on the day of reckoning, but for now, at least they had his dog. Chaz felt comfort in that as he approached his wicked counterpart.

Winston had just finished letting off a shot that struck the dog in its hind leg, blowing it completely off its body. It lay a half step away from Ringo who was now whimpering on the ground in anguish. "The nigger's got a three-legged dog now," Chaz giggled as if the animal's life meant absolutely nothing.

Winston looked over at him, setting the gun down on the tattered barstool beside him. "That's not why I brought you here," Winston replied, now closing in on the wounded dog.

He opened the locked door of a dilapidated shed a few yards away from where Ringo had been assaulted. As he opened the paint-stripped door, he grabbed hold of a metal cart's handle. He carefully dragged out what was clearly an intimidating homemade explosive device with a countdown clock that was set at ten.

He positioned the bomb between Ringo and his recently disconnected limb before stepping away and motioning for Chaz to quickly join him inside The Bug Club. They slipped in through a blown-out doorframe along the exterior of the long-standing run-down building and Winston extracted a remote from the inside of his jacket. He pressed down gently on the yellow button in the center of the switch as a joyous vibe overtook his expression. They were far enough away to watch the clock start counting down as they both stood silently awaiting it to dwindle to zero.

"Forget about a three-legged dog, he ain't gonna have no fucking dog in a few seconds," Winston whispered, breaking the silence.

As the time ran out, the bomb exploded, sending dog guts flying all over the parking lot. The blast was so powerful that the telephone pole split and collapsed backwards into the forest. The area of the concrete lot where the bomb had been placed was left with a cracked foundation and a crater that was the size of a Volkswagen van. They both rejoiced and hugged—the kind of celebration you might see if your favorite football team had just scored a touchdown.

Once the dust settled and the initial excitement of the explosion had lost its luster, Winston got extremely serious. He looked at the still-smoking destruction out back and spoke aloud, but to Chaz, it seemed like what he was saying was directed at himself.

"Now I've just gotta do the same thing about twenty times bigger," Winston said with a methodical smirk crinkling his skin.

They were both committed to the act one-hundred percent. They knew they'd be doing it, but before they could, there was one especially important thing they needed to accomplish. The plan couldn't be set in motion until they removed one sharp and inflammatory thorn from their collective sides. They needed to get their dicks wet.

The one thing they absolutely weren't doing, under any set of circumstances, was dying as virgins. They didn't want people smearing their macabre legacy with claims that they were just a pair of disturbed faggots. No. They needed to be remembered appropriately for their travesties. Without popping their cherries, they would undoubtedly be tied to the "Incel Movement." The crux of their plot was so much bigger than that bullshit, being deprived of pussy would only muddy the waters. They wanted to be infamous.

With the complexity of their rampage in full swing, there wasn't exactly time or patience to woo a few clams their way. They decided the best way to achieve the task would be to weave another sick subplot prior to the massacre. They'd been thinking about it since summer and decided that the Skeleton Un-formal would be the perfect place. Since no sane girl in their right mind would willingly bed them, they'd have to take the extreme approach: DRUG EVERYONE!

The plan was to break into school before the dance and then tamper with the party's refreshments. They'd invested a sizable amount of attention in eavesdropping on their art teacher, Ms. Mello. She was responsible for orchestrating the school gatherings for Bend Brook High, which, of course, included the Skeleton Un-formal. After a few weeks of concentrated surveillance and stalking, they discovered that drinks for the event had already been purchased and were being held in the refrigeration unit in the cafeteria.

It wasn't hard to find when they broke in. The fridge literally had paper signs with sharpie on the numerous jugs of punch that had "Skeleton Un-formal" scribbled across them. The penmanship was familiar to them, especially the "f" in Un-formal as the duo had seen Ms. Mello issue them plenty of those letters in class.

For reasons that were beyond their understanding, Ms. Mello's f's were always of the lowercase variety. They were distinct in comparison to all the other f's they received from the other teachers. Often times when they had failed to complete a drawing or project, she'd just hand them a blank sheet of paper with the giant "f" on it. Their lack of hard work was starting to somehow payoff…

They chose Rohypnol because it was the only date rape drug accessible to them. Chaz had a plethora of drug connections but they typically sold shit of a more recreational nature. The price was doable even with the amount of drink they had to cover. The connect had it in both the pill and liquid form and they chose liquid because it was a more practical fit.

The mind eraser would have actually been their first choice anyway. It was tasteless and odorless, which meant that no one would be suspicious. Even better than that though, in comparison to some of its other competition, it was a much more gradual release. It took about thirty minutes for it to kick in, whereas GHB was closer to fifteen minutes, and Special K was almost an instantaneous knockout punch.

This was important to them since they wanted to have a selection. If one girl took a drink and hit the floor a minute later, people would catch on quickly and stop drinking, resulting in a more limited selection pool or maybe botching their chances altogether. But with the Rohypnol, they'd be chilling for at least half an hour, plenty of time for them to observe who had a chance to ingest the drink.

Once they'd selected a victim (they decided to each rape the same girl since kidnapping two would be too much of a risk), they could continue the motions of the plan. They'd even made a list of the top female talent that they were hoping would down a glass within the initial window. They researched the entire female class for a few weeks before eventually ranking and rating them. They believed it would hopefully make the decision easier when the night finally came. They would time the event and also take down the names of those not on their list that they'd witnessed drinking, in case they had to make a last second substitution.

After a "winner" took a drink, they'd wait for her to get sick. Their knowledge and research on the subject had told them that most drugged girls, once feeling the effects, would head straight for the bathroom. No girl wanted to barf in front of the entire student body, especially in a party setting.

It seemed fitting that Chaz and Winston would be dressed as their favorite duo of schoolhouse killers initially. If anyone asked who they were, they planned to say their costumes were characters from The Matrix. As much as they despised the silly comparison, it could be an essential lie. One that still allowed them their creativity while also brazenly foreshadowing the future homicides that they aimed to achieve.

They'd stashed a separate set of different costumes in one of the ventilation ducts in the boys' lavatory. These costumes would work more to conceal their identities entirely since they covered both the face and body. Winston had suggested Burt and Ernie, which they ultimately ended up settling on because they felt like they were the least threatening.

They hypothesized that the victim would be more likely to find trust in characters plucked directly from their childhood. Also, they were sexually ambiguous, so it wouldn't look weird when they headed to the girls' room as long as no one saw them coming out of the boys' beforehand…

Once they had their target established, it was just a matter of getting changed discretely and hoping that lady luck was on their side. The exit door they planned to use was in the rear of the girls' bathroom which was connected to the girls' locker room. They viewed this as a nice convenience.

The locker rooms always doubled as restrooms during the big events held in the gym. With that in mind, they crafted the withdrawal strategy. The most accommodating aspect of using that path for the kidnapping was that the exit led right out to the back parking garage. Their car would be waiting nearby outside but tucked carefully out of sight. Once they'd led her astray, they would bring her somewhere nice and quiet. A place where many avant-garde romances had been born long before they had been. They'd take her to their vile, demented playground: The Bug Club.

They'd take turns violating her limp body there amongst the debris, wilted surroundings, and insects. Once they'd become men and ripped the proverbial monkey off their back, they could move closer to their ultimate murder plot. Which is the only reason they wouldn't kill the girl. They couldn't reveal themselves just yet, the whore would die… just not on that occasion.

Whenever they had their fill of drilling her, they'd throw her in the trunk and head back toward the school. There was a bakery down the street that had a big dumpster out back. They could toss her in there like the trash she was. There was a possibility that she might even be so embarrassed waking up drowning in garbage that she would omit the whole memory from her drugged mind altogether.

In their eyes, the plan was gold. They might be eventually suspected of drugging the whole school due to their history of deviance, but that would take time for the authorities to put together. In an effort to elongate that development casting them as suspects, they planned to drink some of the punch afterwards and pass out near the premises to blend casually when they were finished. But they'd have to tread carefully and continue to assess the status of the dance and how it unfolded. They couldn't even know for sure if the bash would still be active later in the evening. Whether it got shut down or not would all depend on if they decided to chalk it all up to kids on drugs or kids getting drugged.

If they could return back to the school grounds without being noticed by anyone, and casually melt back into the scene, then they'd be lumped in with the victims. Naturally, an achievement like that would help with suppressing the natural suspicion they would undoubtedly generate when people got to thinking who the fuck would do something like drug the entire school. It wouldn't matter too much anyway, just one week after, they'd all be too dead to make a difference.

By bullet, blade, or bomb, they were all going to pieces. Every last one of them would just become a footnote of their horrible story. A pinch of extra urine in the bladder of their legend that would help push the stream out a little further than the rest of the spree killers in their perverse pissing contest. Once they got some pussy, that was really all that was left.

ROUGH HOUSE

Lacey sifted through the cupboards looking for what had been escaping her now to the point of aggravation. "Where the fuck is it?" she crooned, pushing aside the sloppily arranged contents of the cabinet in irritated fashion.

"Lacey, pleasssssse! We're hungry!" Jack whined from just outside the kitchen.

"If you don't get back in the basement with the rest of the kids, no one is getting anything. You need to listen this time or I'm turning off the movie too."

Young Jack scampered away down the hall dragging the footie-pajama ends of his Tigger outfit on the rug. Lacey heard the obnoxious stomping of his feet distance itself from her. Eventually, it blended in with the spooky music and monster movie audio track as Jack disappeared downstairs to the children's party in the finished basement.

"Thank God," Lacey mumbled, fishing out her phone from her purse. After pressing a few buttons, she held it to her ear and waited as it rang.

"Yo, what's up, babe?" Danny's sexy voice was music to her ears.

"Hi, baby! Sorry to bug you, but I'm in the kitchen right now and I desperately need my strong man's help," she said in her best seduction voice.

"Anything for my princess."

"Do you know if we have any popcorn?"

"Popcorn? You don't need any popcorn, just wait a little longer, baby, I'll give you something nice and salty when I get home."

"Okay, this is officially no longer hot…"

"What, why?"

"Danny, when you say it like that, it sounds… it just sounds disgusting."

"Jesus, what crawled up your ass?"

"It's just these kids—"

"Ew, what?"

"Not literally, dork, I'm saying, these damn kids just aren't gonna shut up unless I find them some fuckin' popcorn."

"You're the one that decided to run a daycare from home. All those kid's parents are out having fun, and look at you. Stuck at home on Halloween obsessing over snacks. You could be out getting shitfaced with me, but you're hanging around, trying to appease a bunch of autistic dipshits instead."

"You know I could give a shit less about Halloween, I'm a Christmas gal, this is just another day to me. Besides one of us needs to make some money, honey. How else am I gonna pay for these new tits you like to play around with so much?"

"Okay, good point. I'll tell you what, I'll let you continue, hell even expand your services if you promise to upgrade to double Ds next year. How's that sound?"

"Danny, where's the fuckin' popcorn?"

"Top right cabinet above the stove."

"Goodbye."

She hung up the phone with an expression that was tired of his shit and then checked the area above the stove immediately. The lone partially-opened box of Orville Redenbacher allowed her to expel a sigh of relief. An old geeky creep had never made her so pleased as Orville did in that moment.

As she peered into the box, she noticed there was one single bag of the microwaveable snack remaining. Another sigh of relief; one was all she needed to quell the hyper-madness of the minors. She pressed the button on the bottom of the microwave and ejected the door. She unwrapped the popcorn and slowly keyed in two minutes and thirty seconds.

As she closed the door and pressed the start button, the worst feeling came over her. It was like something terrible had happened to someone in her family. She didn't know what or how but she felt it. Or did she? The feeling began to contort inside her, it was a feeling of sickness but she wasn't sure why. As she thought about it more, she realized it wasn't about family, it was about her. It felt like someone was watching her…

She spun around as fast as she could, anxious to dispel the conspiracy she'd invented only to instead validate her guttural instincts. There he stood in all his mortifying glory, God's most malevolent abomination covered in blood, vomit, and shit like it was part of his skin—Edmon Black.

Lacey was cornered and her otherworldly internal

reaction immediately snapped her into survival mode. She didn't believe for one second that it was a prank or a joke, everything inside her explained that she was in grave danger and a swift escape was her only chance at continuing to breath.

She thought about jumping out of the window behind her initially, but it was only open a crack. She knew that he would have her in his clutches before she'd be able to open it wide enough. She had no other alternative but to go for the knife. Lacey extracted it from the wooden block and raised it up with impressive speed, she didn't lack wits or agility but when it came to raw power, she hadn't a prayer against Edmon Black.

As she targeted the kill shot, plunging the thick blade down toward his heart, Edmon's hand shot up and put an end to it. His bulbous fingers wrapped around her wrists as he bent it backwards and snapped it clean in half. The hand side of the snapped limb dangled from her forearm, gushing her hot essence. It still clenched the knife as it twisted through the air, only hanging on by a couple of inches of skin that hadn't been torn through already.

She wanted to scream but before she could, Edmon's hand had found her neck. He violently drove his balding scalp into her head, splitting her face wide open and discharging a few teeth from her mouth onto the floor. She stumbled backwards knocking the calmly grinning jack-o'-lantern down onto the black and white kitchen tile.

As Lacey tried to get her bearings, she looked ahead at the stupid pumpkin grinning at her just as all the air left her lungs. Edmon's monstrous foot accounted for most of her tiny cracking backbones. As Edmon's boot came down the popping and bursting sounds of things going wrong inside Lacey's torso filled his eardrums. He bent over carefully while keeping her pinned down with his leg and grabbed hold of her skull from each side with his unforgiving hands.

He dug his digits under each side of her jawbone and firmed his grip to a point where whatever he was grabbing onto would break before his hold did. Tears surged along with the blood raining out from the gum-holes in Lacey's leaking mouth where her teeth had formerly resided. As the pressure mounted, she finally found time to scream, but her cries were cut short by the tearing of her neck tissue. As her inner flesh-collar became visible, Edmon dug his fingers further down into the newly exposed muscle and arteries. He stared down vacantly at the flesh divorcing in her neckline and felt an elating shot of adrenaline fire off through his body. Some people got superhuman strength when trying to save a life, for Edmon, that had only happened when trying to take one.

He pressed down on her devastated backbone, somehow finding a way to make himself even heavier, and readied himself for one final pull. Lacey's spirit cried for her misdeeds on Earth as it felt existence slipping away with the bursting rip of her jugular vein. The purplish tube flopped down like a limp dick as Edmon transitioned his stance, placing his heel on the back of her exposed spinal column. He twisted from left to right while still pulling up, snapping through the dense bone and churning through the remainder of muscle. A gory bouquet of torn human party streamers showered down as he made Lacey's head and body independent of each other.

Just as Edmon had finalized her bare-handed

decapitation, the popping of the kernels came to a close and a digitized beep symbolized the snacks were now ready. He held onto her head tightly, taking a strange comfort in feeling the twitching facial features fade out. She looked like a cyborg short circuiting.

He gawked at the massive inflated bag of popcorn through the microwave window and tried to recall how she had used the device a few moments earlier. He pressed the bottom button and the door swung open, startling him slightly. He pulled the steaming bag of buttery goodness out and tossed it to the floor. The yellow exploded kernels spilled out into the blood pool that was still increasing from her headless body's fast-pumping output.

He set her head inside the cooking box in the center of the clear glass plating. The melancholic toothless leer that was the last thing to live on her face was then eclipsed by the microwave door closing. Edmon had seen her get the device started easily but he wasn't capable of using a toilet, never mind electronics.

After staring at it for long enough, he just mashed the digital keypad with his bloody hand, and somehow, by the strangeness of Samhain, the microwave began to cook. Within seconds, the blood and flesh subjected to the microwave began to crackle and pop like adding milk to a massive bowl of Rice Krispies. Edmon studied the twirling head as the eyeballs puffed out and inflated, knowing his work was far from done.

**

Jack moved his mouth around, navigating the chilly water in the oversized bucket the best he could. His front teeth had just finished punching through a few weeks prior and he was anxious to utilize them and capture one of the Washington reds that had eluded Crissy, Melvin, and Sara Lee already.

"C'mon, Jack, you're never gonna get it! You've been at it for almost an hour now," Sara Lee whined.

"Yeah, what about that popcorn?" Melvin added.

The thought reentered his mind with a deep impact. Bobbing for apples had distracted him to the point that he'd almost forgot. The thought was enough for him to pause the activity and resume his quest to allow them a snack to relax on the couch with.

"Alright, alright, I'll go get it," Jack submitted, rising to his feet and making his way to the staircase again.

"You said that last time too! No excuses anymore!" Crissy hissed, nearly toppling the long black hat off the side of her scalp.

"It's not as easy as you think. You're supposed to be a witch, but if you wanna see a real witch then come upstairs with me." He waited for a moment to see if he had any takers, "That's what I thought."

He turned his back on them and flung the door open and closed it behind him. He began pogo-sticking his way up the stairs in a manner you might expect Tigger to. Once at the top, he cut the theatrics and raced down the hall, shouting, "Laceeeeeey!"

When he hit the breaks at the doorway of the kitchen, he slid to a halt and used the doorframe to keep his balance. His eyes widened to an exaggerated scope as he digested the disgusting, sick display laying on the floor. Lacey's headless corpse, the river of blood, the soggy popcorn shriveling upon contact with her bodily outpourings.

He was shocked but it all seemed like some kind of prank to him. Lacey was probably just mad at him and wanted to get back for all the whining he'd been doing earlier. She wasn't really hurt. In his six-year-old mind, it was all just some elaborate gag to teach him a lesson.

He walked into the center of the destruction casually, "Okay! I see you finally finished the popcorn! Took you long enough!" he yelled, bending over and picking up a handful of the unnaturally rosy snack. He tossed it into his mouth still believing it couldn't be real with a reaction of disgust. Once he'd moved in closer, the sounds of bursting and sizzling flesh came to his attention just as the bizarre pork-like aroma began to overwhelm his senses.

He turned his attention to the active microwave behind him. "What are you cooking, Lacey? Popcorn's already done…"

As the words left Jack's lips, he received the answer; inside the microwave oven sat Lacey's still spinning head. It had been nuking for a few minutes now and the eyeballs were bulging to capacity. She took one final spin before they detonated like a pair of tiny volcanos upchucking a lava-like soup of cornea stew. The pupil porridge plastered the entire window, obscuring any interior visual.

Jack squealed girlishly and ran in the other direction and collided with Edmon, who had been watching his reaction ominously. His tiny body only came up to the bottom of Edmon's thigh. He ricocheted off him and fell back into the soup of blood and popcorn.

Before he could cry, Edmon's foot came down on his stomach. Jack's face reddened as he struggled and squirmed. As the beastly heel hard-pressed his gut, the contents which he'd put in earlier that night made its way up. The frothing puke was a mixture of undigested candy corn, apple juice, meatloaf, and blood. It shot upward, landing over his nose and eyes. The chunky mess splattered all over his face as he felt a pinch in his intestines and bladder next.

Edmon switched his foot and reapplied the horrific density back on his abdomen. This second step worked in the opposite direction, instead of vomit, he was now literally squeezing the shit out of the boy. A black muck soaked through the ass end of his Tigger suit. As his intestines mashed and his bowel gave way, the writhing and nausea ceased.

Edmon removed his boot from Jack's collapsed abdomen and took hold of the shit-smeared bloody tail of his soft costume. He dragged Jack's unresponsive frame down the hall, leaving a reeking trail of darkness and imprint of death behind them. He stopped at the top of the stairs and stood looking down at the basement door as the sounds of a ghoulish soundtrack rumbled below.

Edmon lifted Jack's drooping body up by the tail and slung him like a bullwhip down the flight of steps. The momentum behind his body exploded through the flimsy frame, sending a barrage of splintered woodchips and shrapnel everywhere.

The carpenter's confetti erupted all over the kids unexpectedly who were serenely sitting on the sofa. Their screams took over. They wanted to speak words and ask if Jack was alright but the hysteria wouldn't permit them.

As the massive gore-caked boots made their way down the steps, the pitch of their shrieks only elevated. When Edmon crept into the playroom, the children spread out. Sara Lee hid behind the washing machine and Melvin kept his distance at the far end of the three-seat couch.

Crissy got so frightened when she saw the sick man that she made a bold attempt to streak past him before he got settled downstairs. It would be her final mistake as Edmon's slim-coated fist connected hard with her undeveloped shoulder. The blow caused the joint knob to dislocate, leaving the end pressed against her skin and knocking her to the cold ground. Edmon stuck his sasquatch sole on her petite pelvis and held down her freshly mangled frame.

"Please, mister, I'm sorry! Please, please, just let go! Let go of meeeeee!" she bellowed as he applied his death-grip to each of her calves.

Edmon started to spiral her thighs and her hip hollows crudely, completing rotations that normal human anatomy didn't allow for. As her insides reversed route and snapped stridently, he began to yank upward as the terrified children looked on in absolute horror. But they weren't the only ones looking…

Through the layer of creepy cobwebs and moldy, fog-coated glass, another pair of eyes watched. They were eyes that weren't repulsed or off put by the destruction and viciousness. They weren't eyes of judgement. They were glossy with a different kind of emotion—subterranean almost. They were peering with a dark thoughtful ecstasy painted upon them. As Edmon tugged again, heartlessly pulling the girl's leg from her quaking cavern, they saw everything they'd dreamed of about that night. They were the eyes of Hershel Hughes.

Hershel stroked his vein clad cock vigorously as the girl transitioned into a numb state of shell-shock. He watched Edmon from the cold exterior of the house as he pulled the second limb off the young girl. Edmon shifted his attention from the legless baby before him to the stupefied young man trying to hide behind the couch still.

He threw one of the lanky limbs at Melvin. The bloody nub smacked the side of his face and knocked him to the ground. His glasses flew off, scraping against the floor in the corner as he started to feel around on the concrete vulnerably.

He wasn't anywhere close to finding them when Edmon used the other red leaking leg and began to smash it into his body feverishly. With each savage connection, the broken bone tip slashed into his face, first shredding his cheeks to ribbons, then opening up gaping holes in his expression.

Blood splashed wildly, some even connected with the window that Hershel was lurking outside of. It created a red room kind of aura that made him feel like he was developing a snuff film, but it was even better; he was watching it live. The merciless beating of the girl's meat against the boy's meat was like a natural Viagra. He beat his dick in unison with each strike Edmon dealt out. The closer Melvin's face looked to raw hamburger, the closer he came to climax.

Suddenly, he erupted like a fire hydrant that was just unscrewed. The shots of lumpy semen filled up the latex Magnum rubber around his cock to the point where it nearly flooded from the top. He specifically wore a condom to avoid leaving DNA behind. He was having so much fun but knew he still needed to make sure he didn't jeopardize the bigger picture. The future. As Hershel regained his bearings, he put his cock back into his boxer briefs and zipped his fly. A little dollop of cum was smeared over the top of his index finger, he stuck it in his mouth and licked it clean.

Edmon finally let go of Crissy's decimated leg. Melvin had stopped breathing long ago but Edmon didn't want to stop until he left him unmade. Any ordinary individual would be spent and exhausted after unloading such a strenuous beating, but all Edmon could think about was what came next.

Sara Lee finally found the courage to flee, she'd been watching the sadistic thrashing, and while her mind had been yelling for her to run, her body just wouldn't cooperate. As her actions were once again controllable, she ran from behind the washer and through the destroyed doorframe.

As her first foot reached the step, it slipped off. She looked backwards and saw Edmon slinking closer toward her. The dread dazed her mind as she regained her footing, his substantial footsteps landing on the concrete floor just a few yards away.

She scurried up the stairs and couldn't help but look back again as she saw his gruesome scowl seep out from the darkness at the foot of the staircase. The flapping meat of his ghoulish lack of lower jaw was stirring madly, and as she pulled away from him, the visual disappeared but the sounds still remained.

Hiding didn't make sense to Sara Lee, while she enjoyed a good game of hide and seek like any child, but playing it with a depraved madman wasn't her idea of fun. She knew that if she wanted to live, the front door was her best chance. She scrambled down the hall and grabbed hold of the knob trying not to scream.

As the door swung open, she was faced with a man she'd never seen before. He looked normal enough that maybe he would help her, but the look in his eyes told a far different story. *Why is he happy?* Sara Lee wondered as things seemed to slow down for her.

Her eyes drifted down further to his swollen pants and the silver serrated blade that was glimmering in front of them. She never bothered to ask for help.

THE BEST KIND OF
HATRED

Jesse walked beside Noah, still a bit perturbed by his juvenile foolishness. Pissing on a grave was about the rudest thing she'd seen him do, which meant things weren't getting better, they were getting worse. All the future talk was beginning to seem pointless. Jesse was starting to believe she might be outgrowing their relationship. He had many qualities she enjoyed, but it was coming into focus that there were just some things they weren't going to see eye to eye on.

"Look, I said I was sorry, I'm just getting a buzz, you know, like kids do on Halloween?" Noah wasn't making anything better by blaming it on the drink.

"It's fine, I'm over it. I'm sure that lady's family wouldn't be over it, but what's done is done."

Jesse dragged her fingers against the coarse stone wall of the church they were passing. The area was surprisingly quiet, not that it was the center point of town or anything, but they would've expected more people out and about on Halloween. Jesse withstood a moment of misery; the kids just didn't care anymore.

As they rounded the corner reaching the front of the house of worship, Jesse gawked at the mesmerizing murky cobalt sky. On the rooftop of the longstanding gothic structure sat a finely chiseled gargoyle. One that appeared just a touch more preserved than the rest of the bristly stacked rocks that comprised the spiritual structure.

Its fangs were pointed and perilous, as were his trifecta of ribbed horns. Its muscular and beastly form and build popped out from the blackness, bracketed by widespread wings of wickedness that looked scaly to the touch. The features were flawless and the detail was magnificent, almost a little too magnificent.

"Wow, it's beautiful," Jesse commented, still taking in the breathtaking realism of the stone monstrosity.

It took Noah a moment to understand what the hell she was referring to, "I'm not sure that's exactly the word I'd choose. It's definitely interesting though…"

"Ain't nothing beautiful about that fuckin' demon, let me tell you," Junkie Jim took another sip from the tip of the Evan Williams sticking out the brown bag glued to his hand.

Both Jesse and Noah were startled by his presence. No one was in the area moments ago; it was as if the filthy transient materialized out of nowhere. As he continued to stagger out from the alley beside the church, they paused. Not that they wanted to talk to the rotten-gummed bum, but it seemed harmless enough.

"What do you mean?" Jesse asked, humoring him.

"I mean, that thing's a collector, and for those deserving of being taken, well, let's just say it doesn't end pretty. But everyone's gotta fuckin' die someday, right?"

"I guess so, man…" Noah wasn't sure what else to say to the stranger.

"You might not be so sure if it came down here, if you've seen all it can do to a man. His eyes are filled with the best kind of hatred. The kind that spawns action. You see those claws, and teeth, and wings? That ain't no way for a man to leave this Earth," Junkie Jim explained. "He'd tear the tits right of your little Bessie there, pull those little flesh bags off her, and eat 'em right up. He'd probably fuck her too. I know I would, and see me and him, we got similar taste," he cackled, stirring up a rubbery phlegm rope that expelled from his mouth and slid down his greasy chin.

"Fuck you, you dirty piece of shit," Noah yelled, taking a step closer.

"I see it in your eyes, you ain't no man. A fella like you is all presentation, you puff out your chest like you have intentions of violence, but, motherfucker, before you say another word, just remember that violence you're thinking about I already lived it. I got nothing left but bad intentions," Junkie Jim grabbed the Evan Williams bottle by the neck and smashed it against the stone wall beside him. The sharpened bottle neck sliced open his hand, the now blood-coated glass weapon he brandished twinkled under the streetlight.

The look in Noah's eyes said it all, Junkie Jim wasn't good at most things, but he could sniff out a pussy with the best of them. Whether it be the one between a woman's legs or all-talk afterthought standing in front of him at that very moment.

"Your move, pretty boy, I've opened up more men than the hospital, one more don't mean a goddamn thing to me."

Noah's cowardice left him frozen, looking at the gory glass left thoughts of what diseases might be running through the deranged junkie, clouding his mind. His girlfriend's honor all of a sudden didn't seem that important anymore.

Since Noah was awestruck, Jesse took the initiative, "Sir, we're really sorry, w-we didn't mean anything by it. We're just trying to get to the dance and it's gonna be starting soon, we're just going to leave now. No hard feelings, okay?"

"See, you the smart one, but this little fuck-boy was a cunt hair away from a closed casket. You go have fun at the dance, but don't forget what I told ya, he's watching…" Junkie Jim replied, looking up at the statue again.

"C'mon, let's go," Jesse yelled, snapping Noah out of his daze. They both ran up the street as fast as they could and didn't look back.

PUNCH DRUNK

Edmon saw an open door and walked inside. The gymnasium looked remarkable. It was décor galore; dozens of hand-carved maniacal pumpkins encircled the immense rectangular area. A plethora of fun exaggerated expressions, ranging from creepy to happy to rotten were all present. The tables were filled with various munchies. From finger-food to sweet treats, it was all accounted for. The drink selection was a school dance staple that never seemed to get tired. Enormous bowls of punch sat everywhere, offering fictitious-flavored colors like electric apple, yellow lime pus, and burgundy blood.

Black and orange balloons dotted the whole floor and smoke machines were set around the sides but had yet to be activated. Even though there was no one inside at the moment, the lights were dimmed as if it was time for people to start dancing.

Strobe lights bounced off all the walls, the shapes twisting and morphing constantly in all directions. The twirling disco ball in the center was the pinnacle of the remarkable display. The orange and red Christmas lights running all about the borders and over the top of the room were also a great touch that left the place oozing with an unsettling aura.

There was even a stage near the far wall that had been erected, presumably for the best costume contest. The effort Ms. Mello had put in had to have been a full workday at least. The people that were set to show up would soon be thrilled and in for a memorable evening.

What made it all even more sinister and eerie and gave it the true feel that it was Halloween night was the collection of extremely realistic figures that encircled the entire gym. These were not just some thrown together mannequins with dollar store costumes on, these were highly disturbing horror classics. They had everything from the Wolfman to Michael Myers to aesthetically credible hordes of zombies. The attention to detail and level of authenticity was jaw-dropping.

If Edmon had the mind or mouth to do so, he surely would have. Instead, he just stared at them with imbalance embedded in his eyes. An uncertainty and retardation that was anything but the giddiness you'd expect the typical halfwit to exude in this atmosphere. Most would be prancing around like someone told them they were going out for ice cream, and maybe a few would be the harsh reverse. Terror stricken, crying for mommy, hiding their pupils.

Edmon, like always, was none of the above. He was directionless, detached, and although the way his mind functioned didn't allow him to follow any of it, he was evil. In fairness, his malevolence was the result of the choices of other people, the darkness leeching inside him wasn't organic or self-invented. Nonetheless, he was the picture of wickedness, the unmerciful snuffer of souls. He was… thirsty.

He made his way up to the punch bowl and hoisted the whole thing up with both hands. He poured the tainted drink down his throat, the absence of his lower jaw made for some slippage, but overall, he ingested it surprisingly well. He seemed to enjoy the drink a great deal and quickly moved forward to a second punch bowl. The same similarly sloppy motions were again executed, and he finished the second bowl, tossing it back on the table.

Next, Edmon lingered for some time, staring at the party favors like they were a Magic Eye image. Once he concluded his lethargic exam, he began mashing up some of the cake slices that were tossed on plates sitting on the table beside him. He felt the need to crush them inside his still smelly, blood-drenched, shit-smeared hands since he lacked the ability to chew. The process took a few minutes for each bite to prepare. Patience was never Edmon's strong suit but he was feeling strangely relaxed at the moment. Similar to how he used to feel before getting his diaper changed.

His minimal intelligence was making a surprise appearance, he'd cracked the code! He'd found a way to make the food edible for a man missing his lower jaw. After pulverizing the pastry awhile, he was able to push the fluffy and sugary treat down his feeding hole. It wasn't like the Ladd Institution where they'd bring him a bowl of mush daily, he was having to do some things for himself now.

Suddenly, the sound of a door shutting from the other end of the gym rang out into the empty room, catching Edmon's attention. He walked over to the steel barrier and pushed the handle, but it wouldn't budge. Edmon could almost effortlessly knock most doors right off the hinges, but this one was a little bit more secure than your average door. With school shootings being all the rage the last few decades, any entry point was looking closer to military-level security nowadays.

Also, after drinking all the punch, Edmon was starting to move in a more sluggish manner. He looked off, like he was maybe tired or drunk or… drugged. He headed back over behind the table where the eclectic cast of horror figures stood. When his massive body fell, he landed in a small corner of the gymnasium, directly behind the array of sinister figures. A cozy little spot that was completely out of sight from the rest of the room.

THE HANDLER

Hershel removed the hypodermic needle from the janitor's neck as his lifeless body crumpled to the ground. He'd just finished locking Edmon inside the gym before heading to the car to retrieve some goodies. He'd had an epiphany about what might occur in the school that evening once Edmon walked into it. His premonitions provoked him, whispering in his ear that the next thing he needed was access.

He had followed the janitor into the locker room just as he'd finished purging a load of trash bags. He knew he'd be needing to open those doors in the gym back up again soon, as well as a few others. That's where his new dead friend came into play.

He removed the keyring from his pants along with all of his clothing. He looked at the name tag that read "Skip" before tearing it off. "What a terrible name," he huffed, quickly buttoning up the weathered blue shirt.

"Woooo, don't you wear deodorant?" he scoffed in the direction of the corpse. His displeasure with the scent of body odor overwhelming the garment was clear, nevertheless, he still had to suit up in his nasty rags. He stuffed the clothing he'd stripped off into his duffle bag and upon finishing, he stuffed Skip's dead body into the open locker in front of him. He closed the door and snapped a padlock on it. He didn't want anyone discovering Skip before the festivities began.

Hershel ran down the halls illuminating his statue of liberty ball-cap with the LED lights in it. The savvy sadist was always wary and cognizant of any running cameras. The office was locked but empty, which he was thankful for since he now had Skip's keyring which allowed him access to every room in the building.

It didn't take him long to locate the security system once he unlocked the door. For Hershel, deactivating the system was effortless, his knowledge and expertise with surveillance technology was intricate. He'd seen and operated countless systems, and his practice at the malls made him all the more ready for the winging-it kind of opportunity he was attempting to cash in on.

Once he'd crippled the electronic eyes, he quickly snatched up the duffle bag and made his way back to the gym. The halls were still barren but people would be surfacing soon. He needed to act speedily but also very cautiously. He approached the gym door with angst bubbling, looking through the narrow strip of glass pane that offered him a peek inside. Edmon was nowhere in sight…

He quickly analyzed the area, a little confused as to where he might have gone. Was he hiding? There were so many ghoulish effects in the area, he could easily be camouflaged; a chameleon for all things disturbed.

Hershel made his way through the area and just as he was moving back toward the refreshments, he heard it. The disgusting sound of his wheezing and dangling wrinkly skin flapping were unmistakable.

Hershel worked his way around the edge of the display and saw Edmon lying flat on his back out cold. He slept like a baby, yet was still as hideous as the day he was born. Everything was somehow falling into place like the Devil himself was aligning the portals for him. Edmon was asleep for now but Hershel knew he'd be waking up. If the timing worked out, it would be in a room jam-packed full of youth and he imagined he might react in an… unpredictable way.

He needed to act swiftly for it to come together. He couldn't have been more excited that Edmon chose to wander into Bend Brook High. Having a niece that was attending the school currently, and three daughters who'd graduated there, he was well aware of the annual Halloween bash. He was well aware of how many young children looked forward to the high school's thoughtful celebration of wickedness. The potential bloodshed and destruction would be like nothing he'd ever witnessed.

It was also helpful that he was familiar with the layout from attending events. Hershel found a number of great vantage points that would send a live stream, virtually placing him smack in the middle of the carnage. He set up five tiny high resolution hidden cameras from his pre-packed kit in the boot of his car.

The trunk was always filled with a nice spread of the tools of his demonic trade, a preparation tactic he'd invented to allow him the flexibility to complete a job at the drop of a hat. Never before had he been more thankful for implementing that practice.

Sure, his young niece, Katrina, was a freshman and would most likely be inside, but she was a small sacrifice to pay for the greater good, the potential mayhem that he planned to nurture and help blossom. Plus, she was kind of annoying and whiny anyway. Watching her become part of an epic splatter sequence wouldn't be the worst thing in the world.

Once he'd completed the camera setup, he approached the front of the wide stage. There was a hollowed-out area underneath for storage, an ideal spot to set the cell-jammer. The electronic jammer was a wonderful device that would ensure that all contact was cut off from the inside of the school to the outside world. Once they were trapped, any external contact would be crippled, and soon, their bodies would too, or worse…

The only landlines in the school were located in the office, which had already been locked. It didn't matter anyway; he'd be cutting out all the power to the building when the moment was right. He'd installed a small remote-initiated slicing clamp that was gently nestled around the electrical lines outside.

This meant if he really wanted to let the fright surge to a volcanic scope, all he needed to do was push a button. It was for times like this that all the cameras he worked with had night vision adaptability. He would see them but they wouldn't see Edmon.

He removed an unmarked can of spray from the duffel bag and proceeded to spray heavy coats of the clear liquid on all of the pull switch fire alarms. He waited for about a minute before pulling down with all of his might to test his work. They were now immovable. Another invention with bad intentions that he created the formula for. The ultra-fast drying, unbreakable sealant had bonded to the alarm, rendering it unable to be activated. He'd successfully built a complete wall, stifling any possible ability for outside contact.

Once enough of the teens filed into the belly of his deathtrap and things calmed down for a bit, Hershel would ensure all the exits for the gym were sealed from the outside. It would just be the kids and Edmon, and they would be forced to become acquainted with each other. Society versus its own abomination. Hershel's hardened cock and his watchful eyes.

He prepared himself to exit and make his way to his Cadillac. He'd monitor the influx of party-goers from the parking lot. He'd wait for the most opportune moment to spring into action and lock them inside with the fate he'd chosen for them. Hershel lit up a Newport again on his way outside, pulling in a lengthy drag as a reward for a job well done. He couldn't wait for the party to get started.

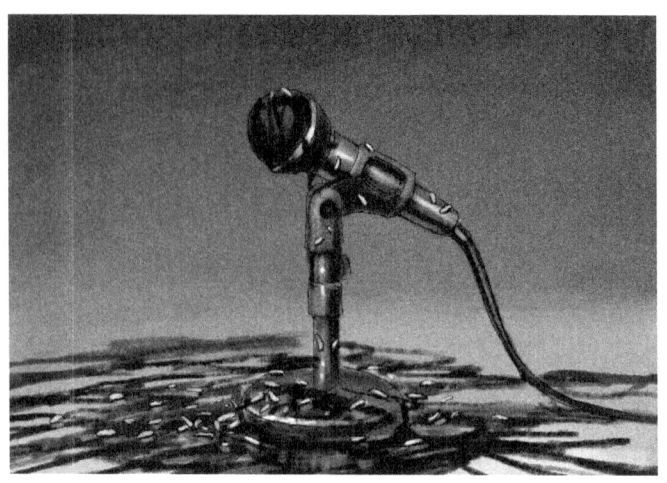

I GOT A FEELING...

Ms. Mello was dumbfounded when she approached the tables to see a couple of empty punch bowls staring back at her. "Jen, I thought you said you filled all the bowls?" she asked her Social Studies counterpart. She listened intently for a moment, believing she'd heard someone wheezing or having trouble breathing before receiving the response.

Jennifer was across on the other side of the gym fiddling with the music output and the PA system. "What?" she yelled back, skipping the remainder of the record spinning by alternating to the other turntable. The Rockwell classic, "Somebody's Watching Me" blared over the speakers, bleeding out the classic lyrics plagued with paranoia for the both of them to enjoy.

The strange inhaling audio had suddenly vanished, overlapped by a much more nostalgic, appeasing soundtrack. The funk retro synths and thumping drums took hold of Ms. Mello. She started to boogie by herself for a moment, being brought back to the time when it was her dressed up as the kid headed to the Halloween party.

"Nothing, forget it," she yelled back over the music. She dropped down below the table, pushing the lengthy black draping tablecloth to the side. She pulled out another jug of punch and began to fill up the bowls again.

"You will all drink from the blood, my pretties. Hee-hee," she laughed in her best creepy voice. Once the dishes were filled, she headed back toward Jennifer who was letting the soundtrack run at a lower level and had moved onto the PA.

"Hey, head up to the microphone, we need to do a quick check, we have to open the doors in ten. If we can get this out of the way, then we're good to go!" she yelled over to Ms. Mello who changed her focus from her over to the stage on her right.

She jogged up to the black microphone stand and grabbed hold of it. "So, what do you want me to say? Is this good? Check. Check," she adlibbed her words, unsure of how to really handle a soundcheck.

"I need you to keep talking. I'm going to be messing with the sound levels for a few minutes, so like, consistent talk, pllllleeease," Jen directed in her best valley girl impression.

"Well, what? What do you want me to say?"

"Anything, just keep talking."

"This is weird, I don't know what to say. You would think it would be easy, but it's really not."

"Jesus Christ, it's not that difficult. Since you're so stressed for a topic just do fuck, marry, kill. Freddy Kruger, Jason Voorhees, or Michael Myers?"

"Oh, my God! That is so good, did you just think of that now?"

"Yeah!" Jennifer said, continuing to tweak the levels.

"Fuck is super easy, Michael all the way."

"What!? Why?"

"He's just so mysterious, like I wanna know, I just wanna know him and feel him. Plus, I think he has the nicest skin out of the three of them," Ms. Mello replied, really taking the query seriously.

"Yeah, but I bet Jason has a bigger cock. Foreskin is the only skin I care about, if you know what I mean." She offered a skanky wink.

"Eww, you're such a gross slut, Jen. Jason is one hundred percent my kill."

"Wait, what? So, you're marrying Freddy?!"

"I like a man with personality, sure he's a burn victim and creepy, but he's funny as hell."

"You realize Freddy's a pedophile… right?"

"Eh, pedos need some love too though," she replied, returning the wink Jennifer's way.

"What the hell are you two talking about?" A booming masculine voice came walking from around the display.

Caught off guard, Jennifer whipped around to see where the comment was coming from. "Principal Richards! Oh, you're early! We were just, ah… finishing up with the soundcheck. Everything's looking like it's good to go!" Jen fiddled with the knobs, putting on a dog and pony show to detract from their politically incorrect jokes.

He squinted his eyes at the pair, judging them. "Alright, I guess it's about time I open up the doors then."

LOCKDOWN

Hershel flicked the burning filter out onto the asphalt and popped the trunk of the Caddy. The remainder of the kids had just finished marching their way inside, without question, eager for the party to get kicked off. The Skeleton Un-formal was an exclusive event for the teens and one of the most exciting moments of the year. Those young ones loved Halloween, Hershel could see it painted on their faces and crafted in their costumes, and it was time for him to cap off the party.

Based on the school layout, there were seven prospective exits he had to account for. The one that led from the gym to directly outside and the two that were on the far side of the gym that piped back into the school were the first he would hit. Those were the second-floor exits.

There were two other doors that led down into the boys' and girls' locker rooms, which he would leave untouched. Those gave access to the restrooms that the partygoers would be using but there were other exits to be mindful of.

Two that funneled out into the parking lot in the rear of each locker room and also another entrance for each that led directly back onto the first floor of the school. Hershel slid another couple of cans of his trusty homemade, black-market bonding agent into his pants and headed into the building.

When he advanced upon the main exit to the outside that everyone had arrived through, he peered inside through the thin strip of clear window. Everyone seemed to be having the time of their lives. It looked like a couple of adults were inside right near the doors, monitoring if anyone tried to leave or come inside. He gave a gentle tug on the door and opened it without attracting any attention. He sprayed a heavy amount of his bonding agent into the locking mechanism and quietly closed it.

Next, he made his way around the building and in through the side exit which he unlocked with Skip's keyring. This entrance now gave him close access to the four entry points he needed to hit. Those doors had already been locked by administration presumably, so no one was standing guard by them. No matter, he wasn't taking any chances. He unlocked each door manually and sprayed another generous coating before closing them shut. He still didn't know if someone inside had a key to them.

On the third door, he slipped inside the girls' locker room before sealing it. He had to first ensure that the interior exit was accounted for beforehand. He was hoping no one had to piss yet since the crowd had just arrived as he crept in cautiously. The room was barren, he was able to seal the rear exit and quickly followed up with the entrance. Now that the females had been assured no chance of escape, the males were next.

Upon entry, he again stealthily tiptoed straight to the rear door. Not seeing anyone within his immediate radius, he smoothly opened the door and loaded up the lock with the clear adhesive substance. As he closed the exit, he heard either a toilet or urinal flush. Hershel flashed around, meeting the stern and scrutinizing glare of Principal Richards.

"Who are you?" he demanded.

"Name's Hershel, Hershel Hughes, sir."

"Why are you in my school?"

"Skip sent me, he couldn't make it in today. He got stuck."

"What do you mean stuck?"

"Stuck, like stranded. Said his car broke down and he's waiting for triple-A out on ninety-five. He just wanted me to take care of a couple of things before the big bash and all. Make sure the kids still have a hell-of-a night and all."

"Well, he doesn't have the authority to just give anyone he wants keys to the school. You can't just come in here and work without consulting anyone. What are you doing to my door?" Principal Richards' agitation with the explanation continued to grow.

"Oh, this is just a little ol' WD40. The Skipper said that this door was having some issues and he wanted to make sure the emergency exits were up to snuff for the kids. Said it was urgent since it's a violation of fire code."

"I'm afraid I'm going to have to verify that you should be here before I can let you go," he explained, removing the cell phone from his pocket and dialing.

Hershel grinned cynically, his blonde teeth popping out into the open. "Not a problem, boss, I'm with you. We've gotta do whatever we have to do to make sure these kids are safe."

As the phone rang into Principal Richards' eardrum, the opposite one picked up another ringing that was almost synchronized with the number he'd dialed. The ringing sounded like it was coming from a locker that was only a few feet away from them. A terrible feeling suddenly pounded Principal Richards in the gut.

"What the hell… Skip! Skip, is that you?" Right as Principal Richards finished his question, Hershel leveled the dual canisters at his crinkly face and pressed down. The thick clear mist saturated his head and he speedily turned away, attempting to shield himself from any further oncoming attacks. Hershel found another opening reaching around him and spraying upward, again, nailing him with an even thicker second coat.

"My eyes, I… can't…" His speech began to slur and his eyelids steadily slowed their movement, freezing in an almost completely closed state. His other limbs still moved at normal speed, but his face had deteriorated into a petrified version of the shock stewing within him. It was now there forever, or at least until his expression rotted away altogether. Hershel extracted another hypodermic needle from his pocket and pulled off the cap.

He plunged it deep down into Principal Richards' neck, an area that he'd been vigilant not to solidify with his solution. He drove the thin metal into his flesh and propelled the lethal contents of the injection tube into the principal's bloodstream. To Hershel's relief, he fell dead to the ground only a few moments after what turned out to be his final booster. He didn't want to be down there too long since there was no telling when someone was going to pop in and take a leak. He needed to be gone by then. He needed to move fast.

It wasn't him who was supposed to be stacking bodies, he wanted to be back in the bowels of Bedlam, watching Edmon awaken, with a tub of lube beside him. "Guess now would be a good time to activate the jammer," he exhaled, pocketing the dead man's cell phone. He felt a little foolish for not doing so prior to the principal's call. He rolled up his arm sleeve and activated the wrist remote comprised of about a dozen or so buttons. Once the lights illuminated, he pressed a triangular yellow button.

The cell jammer under the stage upstairs responded with a dot of green light bringing it to life. Hershel picked up Principal Richards' limp corpse and dragged him into the bathroom. He propped him up inside one of the bathroom stalls and shut it behind him. He was able to escape the boys' locker room without further incident. He applied the bonding agent to what was now the school's last remaining entry, just as he finished passing through it.

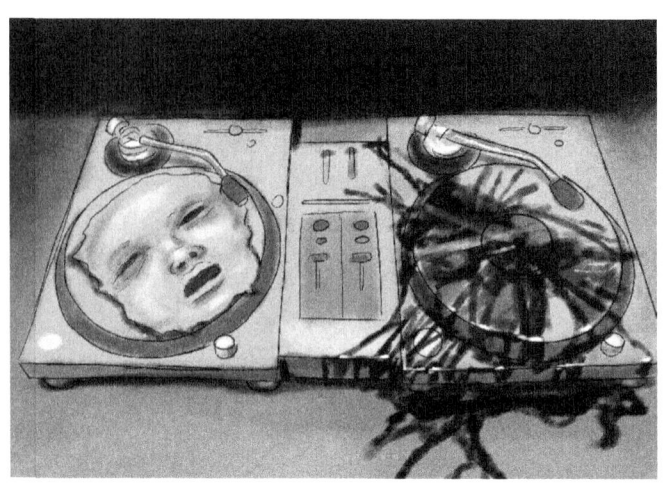

DANCE OF THE DOOMED

The place was packed to capacity—lights flashing, costumes glowing, and delight abound. This is what they'd waited months for, everyone was there to partake in the surreal moment. Ms. Mello stood by the door watching Jen across her room snap her head back and forth while a pair of headphones hugged it. Something about a white woman in her late thirties playing DJ so passionately was highly comical to her.

That was her costume, but still, there was a small part of her that believed she wasn't acting. This was some kind of hidden dream. Her doing a pull-back scratch during the hook of the Ghostbusters theme song only hardened that belief.

Ms. Mello had changed into her classic Bride of

Frankenstein costume just before the party started. Her hips poked out a bit in the dress but she still looked hot. She was the epitome of the kind of teacher that horny teens fantasied about boning. An impossible feat, a fictional daydream for nearly the entire student body. Everyone except Charles Buckley that is.

Charles was dressed up as Zorro. He thought the classic costume looked funny on him. Zorro had never been an exaggeratedly athletic individual, so his toned frame seemed to not quite align with the spirit of the character. He grabbed hold of Ms. Mello's meaty ass discreetly with confidence, palming nearly the whole cheek. She turned, stunned at first, but then quickly simmered down when she realized whose hand it was.

"Mmmm, hope that is just the beginning," she begged.

"Well, we'll see. If you're a good girl today then, maybe, just maybe, I can give you what you need," he spoke with a solid buoyancy that also displayed his dominance over her.

"Zorro though? That would NOT have been my first guess for your outfit," she giggled, biting at her ash-toned fingernail.

"Why not? Why can't a brother wear a mask that doesn't involve holding a gun at a gas station at 3 AM? You on some racist shit," he teased.

"If there's one thing I've learned about you, Charles, it's that you love fucking too much to ever risk having your freedom taken away."

Charles didn't really absorb what she was saying. He couldn't respond to the odd compliment since his attention drifted off into the crowd. He stared blankly, thinking to himself.

"Hey, what's wrong, sexy?"

"Ringo still hasn't come back. It's just not like him, he's never been away from the house for more than a few hours. Sorry, I know that probably wasn't what you were expecting me to say. But I'm starting to think he's never going to come back." The pain in his expression was of the heartbreaking variety.

"I'm sure he's just taking a little doggy vacation. Sometimes dogs need that too. He'll be back, I know he will," she tried to reassure him.

"I don't think he left on his own."

"You think someone took him? Who do you think would do something like that?"

"I have my suspicions."

***

Chaz and Winston were perched in the far corner leaned up against the wall. They'd found a relatively low populated area that allowed for an unobstructed view of the entire row of tables. The punchbowls were their focus, and Winston had a small moleskin journal and pen out. He discreetly made note of each girl that indulged in the beverages they'd loaded with the liquefied date rape drug.

"Can you believe that fucking nigger is tagging Ms. Mello? I really wish it was him that was rotting in the ground right now instead of his worthless mutt."

"Don't worry, he'll be the first to get waxed next week. Tonight, though, I need you to focus on the slit list, not the shit list or the hit list, okay, buddy boy?" Winston instructed, refocusing him on the task at hand.

"Right, so who do we have so far?"

"Ruby Harris?"

"Love the face but her torso reminds me of SpongeBob SquarePants. It's weird."

"Fair enough, Jasmine Patel?"

"I'm not fucking no sand-nigger, I heard their pussies smell like Casey Anthony's trunk."

"You don't think she's hot? No one's saying you have to have a baby with her, we're just raping her, dude." Winston tried to reason; Jasmine's sexy female form seemed to outweigh his racist life views.

"Next," Chaz said, putting the kibosh on what Winston believed to be a viable option.

"Sandy Sousa?"

"Skank."

"Cindy Joyner?"

"Dead fuck."

"What do you mean?"

"Tim Lansdale told me that. Said she's like a corpse in the sack, doesn't move at all."

"Dude, they're all gonna be dead fucks, we're knocking them out, for Christ sake! Do you have any idea what's going on here?" Winston's irritation with his idiocy was starting to boil.

"Yeah, but I'm just saying like, if she happened to wake up or whatever, and she was into it, you never know…" Chaz defended.

"I'm not even gonna touch it, you're… you're such a retard, dude. All I know is we need to pick one soon, they are going to start dropping like flies out here."

"OKAY! OKAY! Who's next?"

"Sara Hunter? What's wrong with her? Does she have a Jewish uncle or a sixth toe? I'm just dying to hear what you're gonna trudge up for this one," Winston barked, waiting for him to respond. "Well?"

"She's it, brother, she's the one. She's been a cunt

to us in the past too, so this will be extra sweet."

"Alright, Sara Hunter it is, she's hot as shit, bro!" Winston said as the pair high-fived. "Well, my notes indicate that she took her first sip about twenty minutes ago so we need to move fast. Let's go get changed now!"

Chaz gave him a stark, evil look as they locked pupils, "Let's rape this bitch."

They both headed towards the boys' locker room where they'd stashed their second outfits. As they passed through the crowd, they brushed into Jesse and Noah on the dance floor.

"Hey, watch where you're going, asshole!" Noah yelled as they bumped into them, nearly causing him to lose his footing.

"Go find a boyfriend, art fag," Chaz remarked back, throwing up a bird in passing.

"Those mother fu—" Noah was interrupted by Jesse who was disgusted by his overcompensation. He was trying to play the badass again, possibly make-up for bitching out against Junkie Jim. But it was so painfully obvious that acting like the tough guy was the last "role" he could pull off, on or off the stage.

"Forget about them, let's take a quick break," Jesse suggested.

She planted a kiss on his lips. She didn't do it because she was aroused, it was an effort to pacify things. Kissing him would help them both forget about the bullshit that had started their night off so poorly. More than anything, she just wanted to have a good time and bring home that award.

Despite the earlier nonsense, Jesse and Noah had shaken most of the evening's downward spiral off. They were the first ones on the dance floor, boogieing down to the eerie tracks ejecting from the speakers around them. Jesse wanted to avoid perspiring too much and preserve her costume make-up quality before it started dripping down her face. The contest usually happened early on in the night and she didn't want to alter her prime, unspoiled appearance.

The break was long overdue, there were so many cool decorations that deserved a closer look. She was impressed by how the faculty had come together to outdo last year's nearly equally impressive shindig. She felt really fortunate to be at a place like Bend Brook High where the teachers didn't get much credit but they were always there to make sure the students had super quality events.

"Babe, I'm gonna get a drink, you want one?"

"No, I can't risk messing up the make-up yet. I'll just have one after the contest but I will join you over there. I wanna check out those gnarly figures. Do you see the Pumpkinhead replica?" she asked, pointing it out. "It's obviously nowhere near as tall but it still looks almost identical. Remind me to ask Ms. Mello where it came from later."

"Right on, babe," Noah said as they both got closer to the table. She looked again through the row of evil pumpkins and the variety of strange figures. A creepy scarecrow loomed over the punch bowl and as they advanced, it jumped forward at them while screaming. Noah spilled the solo cup he had partially filled before cursing it. "Fucking animatronics! I definitely wasn't expecting that."

Jesse chuckled before reminding him, "CGI can't do that, can it?"

Noah smiled back at her, not objecting to the point. "Well played, well played as usual. Let me ask you then, which one is your favorite?"

Jesse thought about it carefully, turning around at first and gliding her gaze in a panoramic fashion back through all of the figures until she was brought back to the ones in front of her again. There was one particular figure that stood out uniquely on its own. One that was highly realistic that she hadn't noticed before. One that must have been animatronic as well because it looked and sounded like it was breathing. One that had no lower jaw, just a collection of flesh flapping and scattering around the area. One that was so massive it almost looked like it was on stilts. One that created a certain amount of unease within her, something that no other costume ever had. She didn't know why and that bothered her. She LOVED IT.

"I'm not sure if favorite is the right word, maybe soul mate is better? But that creepy thing, I've never seen anything like that before."

Noah turned in the direction that she was pointing, having not really noticed the figure as it blended in well with the rest. "Pretty gruesome, should we go in to get a closer look?"

Before Jesse had a chance to answer his question, an announcement came on over the PA: "Okay, I want to ask everyone to please line up near the stage, it's time for us to cast our vote on the best costume of the night!" Ms. Mello's voice rang out excitedly through the distorted speakers. Everyone immediately started to huddle around the stage area, surrounding her.

"C'mon, this is it!" Jesse shouted, dragging Noah away from the table.

"But I didn't even get a drink yet," he whined.

"AFTER!"

Noah followed her obediently knowing now wasn't

the moment to test her. No matter how insignificant the silly contest seemed to him, Noah knew it meant the world to Jesse.

"I'm going to call up the top three costumes that we've decided on, and then we are going to ask each of you to cheer for your favorite. Loudest response gets… forget about last year's 25, this year, the winner gets a 50-dollar gift card to Dunkin' Donuts!" The crowd cheered mockingly at the prize. "Hey, guys, that's like ten Coolattas, are you kidding me?" she defended.

"Okay, so first, no surprise here, Jesse Cage, please come on up!" Jesse wasn't surprised but reacted in a humble, smitten manner nonetheless. Her actions were those of a pro.

Noah cheered her in an overtly biased manner as she ascended the stage and stood beside Ms. Mello. She grimaced ferociously to the crowd's enjoyment, playing on the costume convincingly. She didn't really need to; they were already enamored with it.

"Alright, and for those who don't know, what are you, Jesse?"

"I'm Sil, from Species!"

The crowd let out a thunderous applause, it was clear that it wasn't going to get any louder than when it started, but still, they needed to play out the formality and give all a fighting chance.

"Okay, next I wanna call up, Devan Kelly!"

Devan was dressed up as Freddy Krueger and the gimmick looked pretty good, but the originality and hands-on touches were severely lacking. He had all the appropriate elements to the costume purchased but none of the heart that Jesse's oozed with. The cheers were minimal, the audience was far from authentically impressed by the get up. They were just being polite.

"Fuckin' fag!" a random young man in the audience called out in booming voice.

"Hey, language, people. If I catch another person doing that, you'll be done for the night. DONE FOR THE NIGHT. Alright, and finally, Linda Spencer!" Linda was dressed nearly identical to Wonder Woman. She truly looked like her too, but the disconnect was probably that she looked closer to Lynda Carter, the 1970s version, rather than the updated Gal Gadot variety that everyone was currently drooling over. Not that they recognized Jesse's character either, but they didn't have to. The make-up was just too captivating not to be excited.

"Well, I think we have a pretty clear-cut winner then," Ms. Mello shouted out to the crowd.

Jesse found herself looking through the crowd at the entertained faces and there it was. The same strange figure that she'd been so captivated by just prior to the contest. It stood nearly two feet taller than the biggest kid in their class. The people around the figure seemed to be disgusted, like there was a horrible smell clouded all around them. *A method actor, brilliant,* she thought to herself.

A small circular space had evolved around the figure, almost like a spotlight that only served to allow her to further key in on it. This might have been the best costume she'd ever seen. She wanted to win the contest more than anything that night but she needed it to be an outright defeat against the best competition. She wasn't about escaping with or stealing victories, that wasn't her style. Plus, she had to know who was in the costume. She needed to pull back the curtain on the wizard, to expose the genius…

"And for the third year in a row! Your winn—" Ms. Mello was cut short by Jesse as she whispered into her ear on stage. Ms. Mello nodded her head, a little confused at first, and then confirmed her request again.

"Actually, I stand corrected. This year's potential winner has suggested we do one more rating. It appears we've overlooked a fabulous costume. I'm not sure who's in the mystery costume down on the floor there. The horrific, bloodthirsty ghoul? Is that what you're dressed as? Oh, I see you've ripped through you're strait-jacket too. We have a Ghoul-Maniac! Boys and girls, let's all give a nice warm welcome to the Ghoul-Maniac! Come on up to the stage!"

As Ms. Mello beckoned Edmon to the step-up, DJ Jen was keying up a celebration record that she was just itching to spin. With the added drama of the new costume contestant, she held off, but everything was ready to go by the time Edmon sluggishly dragged himself up onto the stage.

"Oh, my good God! You really do play the part, don't you? The smell is frighteningly foul."

"He fucking smells like shit!" A random voice belted out. An eruption of laughter echoed, but still, Edmon's reaction was non-existent as ever.

"Hey, knock it off!" she barked at the immaturity emanating from the crowd. "What's your name?" she asked, sticking the mic up toward his still wheezing skin. The crowd could only hear the meat flapping through the PA as they continued their sneering and snickers. He didn't say a word to any of them.

"Okay, I guess we have a real man or woman of mystery here. Everyone, real quick, let's go back to Jesse one more time, give it up!" Ms. Mello's hand hovered over her mutant head while the crowd cheered with roughly the same intensity as they'd done during the prior ask.

"Okay, that's another great reaction for Jesse," she said, stepping a few paces back toward Edmon. "And finally, let's hear what everyone thinks about the Ghoul-Maniac!" The whole building erupted in chaos, there wasn't a single person who wasn't cheering in some capacity, even Jesse. The onlookers couldn't help but gravitate toward Edmon Black.

"Wow, well, it looks like we've got an upset for the ages here. Jesse, I'm sorry, but this year's Skeleton Unformal winner is…" She stuck the mic back up toward Edmon's mouth area, only to hear more of the same. No words just his ghastliness.

"Well, listen, if you want to walk away with the 50-dollar Dunkin' gift card, then you're gonna have to show us the goods, mister. The people are curious… I'm curious," Ms. Mello demanded.

"Who the fuck is he?" A male voice screamed from the audience.

"Hey, keep quiet! No language I said!" she yelled. Jesse couldn't wait for the unveiling; she was chewing on her slimy alien fingernail in anticipation.

Based on Edmon's dark unbreakable character, Ms. Mello had no choice but to give him some assistance, "Looks like you need a little help," she surmised.

She stood on her tippy-toes and reached for the ear closest to her to try and pull off the "mask." When her hand touched his flesh, she quickly tugged, but in seconds deduced that, in fact, it wasn't a mask on his face. The foul frame he projected was something he owned, something he had to deal with outside of Halloween. Something that painted him in a new tragic and disturbing light.

The unexpected texture made her jump and emit a noise like you would if you saw a large spider on your arm. Still, the shock didn't separate her far enough from Edmon. His abnormally docile, drug-induced state appeared to have finally waivered. He recalled how much he didn't like being touched as his instincts ignited again. He recollected the hatred woven deep in his heart for those who'd taken him away from his mother. For everyone.

The repercussion of the move that Ms. Mello had pulled left her instantly regretting that she'd never taken the time to apply for life insurance. Edmon's thumb and index finger slammed into her eye-sockets, but not too far. He worked his dirty digits underneath the lower skin of her face as the crowd looking on screamed in horror.

They weren't quite sure if this was some kind of trick or the real thing yet. Any confusion on that question was cleared up when he ripped her whole face off. The absurd, brute force he initiated peeled it back abruptly. As the skin stripped away from skull's front, a nasty dripping plethora of stringy sliminess dissipated upon the detachment of the face. The freshly created gore cavern looked like one of the human anatomy posters on the wall at the doctor's office. The ripping audio that echoed throughout the gymnasium was loud enough to wake the dead.

Ms. Mello stood shaking with the mushy, chewed-up cherry pulp laid across her face, discharging the warm life right out of her. Edmon tossed the skin-mask away carelessly and it landed on top of the record Jennifer had just keyed up, flipping the switch in the process. Bobby Pickett's classic the "Monster Mash" boomed out from the speakers while she stared down at her friend's face spinning right round on the vinyl. She let out a shriek that could've crowned her the next scream queen.

The room erupted and total anarchy ensued. Kids running for every exit as Edmon grabbed the fleeing Devan Kelly by the neck of his Kruger sweater. He got one hand around his throat and the other on the back of his head and started to squeeze. His eyeballs began to crack with bloody lines and push out of his skull. After applying a little more pressure, they blew out altogether and the back of his skull turned into a pile of slush in Edmon's hands.

Jesse jumped down off the side of the stage, feet flat, not about to twist her ankle like every girl escaping in every horror movie she'd ever seen. What she was witnessing was unbelievable. She needed to get Noah and split, or be split. Everyone headed for the main exit, which by the grace of Hershel Hughes, was not operational. They could also thank him moments later when they pulled out their cell phones and got no service. They were now at the mercy of a maniac.

Edmon had made his way to the middle of the dance floor but had no intentions of partaking in anything aside from ending lives. The mass of students that had realized the exit was not opening would have to go through him if they wanted to get a chance at another escape through the locker rooms.

They ran wildly forward, the way the first line of infantry might during a war, unknowing of how much longer they'd be afforded the luxury of breathing. The first line Edmon slaughtered with ease. He arched one boy backward, the front of the kid's neck buried in his rancid armpit. He bent him slowly over his knee until his spine snapped and a jagged ending was poking out through his stomach region. Once his crippling was complete, he tossed the boy back into the middle of the dance floor.

He wiggled around on the ground, twisting at an angle that made him more look like a deer that had been struck by an SUV than a man. The next boy wouldn't be fortunate enough to remain intact as Edmon grabbed hold of each of his arms and pulled them in opposite directions. His inhuman power saw them pop out of the joints before tearing clean off the frame. He howled out as his fluids rained out all over the buffed sports center surface.

The waves of blood spilling out from his arm sockets opened the door for additional spills to occur. Many of the others making their run for freedom started to trip and stumble their way toward him, which only simplified his agenda.

A hefty girl slid toward him, resembling a cartoon character as she juggled her footing rapidly. Edmon's fist found the blood-spattered zombie waitress's abdomen. Bones crunched and splintered when the blow landed, forcing the girl to lose control of the contents of her bowels.

Her liquid excrement and piss shot down from her skirt and onto the crimson floor below, giving a new visual to the term beating the shit out of someone. The girl stopped breathing and collapsed to the floor, squirming in her own mess. Suddenly, from behind, one of the steel chairs smacked across Edmon's back like a WWF attitude era hardcore match. Edmon turned around as Jennifer cocked the now distorted, potato chip-looking chair back once again.

Edmon swatted the chair out of her hands as she drove it forward, sending it cycling with the speed of a ninja star. It shot across the room until finding the face of a girl dressed like Bart Simpson. The puffy cloth-suited character slumped down against the wall as red began to soak into the costume underneath. Jennifer stared at the body in awe of his freakish assets and in fear for her existence.

Her last thoughts concluded with the realization that her fear was coming to fruition and that her cheap, short-lived revenge wasn't sweet enough to trade her life for. Edmon grabbed her by the neck and bashed her face into the turntables single-mindedly. The primal nature of his actions left her music station in shambles and her face looking like death.

He then scooted over and did the same with the many boxes of records that she'd hauled over with the equipment. By the time he was finished, countless fragments of shattered records were stuck in her face and spread around randomly. The jagged vinyl had sliced deep gashes into some areas and penetrated others. She was unrecognizable when he slammed her down for an explosive final thrashing.

Two kids, dressed like Raggedy Anne & Andy, nearly snuck down behind him into the girls' locker room but seemed to have trouble opening the door. Edmon's elongated arms shot out to them rapidly. The hands clamped around both of their tender teen necks and rag-dolled their bodies forward. He pitched the pair of them into the giant set of speakers near the blood-soaked spin table. Sparks bounced up and around Edmon while the electricity caused their bodies to gyrate violently like seizure victim getting a massage with a jackhammer.

Moments later, the strength of the electric current caused the bodies to begin to smoke and catch fire.

Jesse and Noah, who were relieved to have found each other amongst the mayhem, had hidden on the side of the stage behind the many decorative figures. The same area that had initially guarded the sleepy, previously incapacitated rendition of Edmon.

"How the fuck do the cell phones not work!? We literally use them here every day!" Noah yelled, enraged by the device.

"I don't know, mine doesn't work either," a voice said from behind them. Charles had found their hiding spot and was looking for someone to game plan with. They seemed a little calmer than the flocks of teens burning up their lungs just to get torn apart by the evil they'd been trapped with.

Suddenly, all of the lights in the building cut out. The gym was now only illuminated by the weak glow of the devilish pumpkin faces that encompassed the room and the burning corpses near the DJ setup.

"What happened to the fucking lights?" Noah cried.

Once their eyes adjusted to the dark, they watched through a less vivacious lens, in disbelief, as Edmon continued to tear through the teenagers. The sound of skulls being split and crushed, breaking bones, and bodies dropping only became more pronounced with the dulled visuals. It was repetitive, people were dying left and right. With each second that passed, they watched and listened to a new person being destroyed in vulgar fashion. They were all speechless until Noah finally broke the silence.

"Who the fuck is that guy?"

"I don't think that's really the question that matters right now, I think it's how do we get away from that fuckin guy…"

"What are we going to do, he's… he's going to get

to us eventually, right? When he runs out of people to kill, right?"

"This is a good spot, there is a chance that he might not see us, it's better than exposing ourselves again," Noah replied.

"There's not many people left alive, once he's done with them, he'll come this way, and then what?" Jesse rebutted.

"I think Jesse is right, our only shot is making a run for the boys' locker room. He's still on the girls' side right now. If we move quickly, we have a chance, but this is a short window, we'd have to go now," Charles responded, making his pitch.

"No! We stay here and wait for the police, it's too risky!"

"What fucking police? We just went over this, the cells are useless, you think he's calling the cops?" Charles yelled, pointing at the backwards boy with the arched spine wriggling on the floor still. "I don't have time to debate you, Noah," he looked over to the more like-minded Jesse, "You in?"

Jesse looked at Noah with a nervous gaze, the kind that screamed the end of days was near, "I'm in."

"Alright, we go now then, ready?"

"Wait!" Noah interrupted. They both looked to him waiting. "I'm in too."

"Glad you came to your senses. Let's go!" Charles gave the command which looked ridiculous coming from a black version of Zorro. He was hopeful that one day, under different circumstances, they could have a laugh about this. Edmon had a boy lifted off the ground by his throat, elevated above his own height. His face had gone deep purple and his watery eyes were glazing over.

The last thing they could see in the expiring boy's limp expression was envy, as through the darkness, he watched the three of them sneak quietly down into the boys' locker room.

30 MINUTES
EARLIER

A QUESTION OF
CONSENT

Sara Hunter was starting to feel woozy. It might've had something to do with all the pre-gaming from a few hours ago, drowning in the latest zero-calorie vodka. Whatever the case, a lightheadedness was now in the air. She felt like she might vomit right as Ms. Mello started making her way to the stage. She could tell the costume contest was about to begin.

Sara knew her chances of winning were minimal with her trashier "hot referee" costume, but she still loved seeing them rate the participants and declare the winner. She would have to miss it this time around, her body was giving her no other choice but to head down to the restroom. The last thing she saw before her eyes started to seal shut were two other "girls" following her down in Burt & Ernie costumes.

After slipping on their new disguises, Chaz and Winston made their way into the ladies' room. The timing was ideal, it just so happened that their top draft pick had wandered into the locker room first, while essentially everyone else was watching the reveal upstairs. When they got to the lower level, they scoped out the area and made sure no one was there with them. Once they were able to confirm it was clear, they took aim at Sara. She was slumped over a railing and barely standing when each of them hooked an arm and dragged her toward the exit door.

Chaz pressed up against it and instantly bounced off. "What the fuck? Did someone lock this?" he asked rhetorically in a confused manner.

"They can't lock this, it's a fuckin' emergency exit!" Winston yelled, giving it a try himself.

"This doesn't make any sense…" Chaz replied.

Before they could utter another word, they began to hear a chorus of fear-filled screams roaring upstairs. At first, it sounded like cheering, but as they listened more intently, they could hear a certain terror to the tone that was easily distinguishable. They dropped Sara to the cold floor and rushed up the staircase at once.

When they peered out the small pane of glass, it allowed them a glimpse into the gym. What they saw next both disturbed and thrilled them. Worst of all, it created a gnawing feeling of jealously.

There was someone dressed up like a seven-foot maniac killing everyone in the gym. He was literally tearing people apart, beating them to a broken pulp, and exploding their craniums. They saw Ms. Mello staggering around, missing her whole face, too ruined to react.

"No way, this fuckin' guy is off his rocker!" Chaz exclaimed.

"We gotta get this door locked! What if… what if he comes in here?" Winston chimed in.

There was a set of extra metal chairs that were stacked up in the hallway beside the doorway, both Winston and Chaz alertly started to wedge a couple upward, under the handle of the door. They were able to pin them just perfectly as demonstrated by a duo of students dressed in Raggedy Anne & Andy costumes. They attempted to bull their way inside, evading the maniac, but were rejected by the jammed door.

Chaz and Winston watched as the two were pitched into the speaker system and electrocuted until they were void of life and then some. They looked like bugs that had run into a human-sized zap lamp as their skin cooked and smoke rose off of their flaming costumes. All of the lighting in the building suddenly cut out as Edmon moved back out toward the larger group. The fear within the others caused inhuman noises to be released as the rampage continued.

"So, the way I see it is, we're probably gonna die in here tonight. These chairs might stop raggedy asshole and her pal, but it's not stopping that… that thing," Winston reflected.

"This is bullshit. We were supposed to kill all of them. He's stealing our kills, our bloodshed! That bastard!" Chaz's anger was showing through.

"Well, it's all over now. There's nothing we can do at this point. He's stolen our thunder."

"Actually, there is one thing we can still do…" Chaz replied with a devious smile, waving for his twisted counterpart to follow behind him downstairs.

Sara was still not moving, she laid knocked out cold

on the beige tile floor. They laid her body out near the lockers, over the concrete median that bridged two benches together. Neither of them said a word, they just pulled down her tiny black ref skirt, followed by the neon green thong that covered her slit under it. The captivated pair should have brought a drool cup.

The fun of the event had been stripped for the boys. They both took turns ramming her ruthlessly, trading off back and forth many times. Sara's warm wet snatch felt wonderful against their virgin cocks. One held her legs spread while the other continued fucking and fingering her asshole.

Even as Winston rose to climax inside her, his face remained blank and absent of emotion. After his hot cum filled her violated burrow he pulled out to make way for Chaz. As he picked up where his partner left off it was as if he was just going through the motions. He couldn't help but wonder if his first lay was going to be his last. That's how they planned it originally, but it was no longer on their own terms.

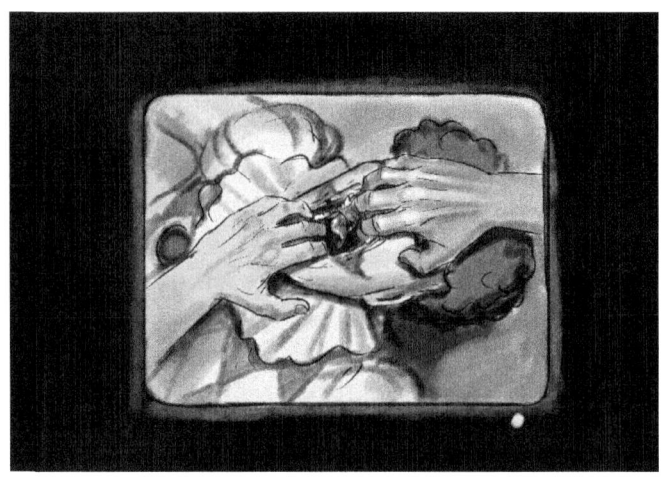

DEAD STREAM

Hershel pressed a small blue button on his remote wristband, and suddenly, all of his monitors went from full color to night vision. As all of the power left the school, he adjusted his position and got a little more comfortable. He laid sprawled out in a small circular bed that he'd temporarily filled the previous kill space with. He was more than enjoying the live stream of Edmon's nefarious activities; the butchery.

He'd just finished watching the maniac pull out the guts of his niece, Katrina—his sacrificial lamb. The child that was his own blood, his family. It made him feel good, like he was contributing too. The indecencies of the evening needed to commence. To him, it was an easy decision and a fair trade.

Hershel had about stroked himself to sleep, he'd never cum more in a single night. Mable slithered around the top tank of the boat around him, watching him binge on the repulsion he'd organized. There was a proud feeling within him like he'd just directed an Oscar-worthy film.

He was recording everything so he'd be able to watch it for eternity, which was good because he'd need to be back at the Ladd Institute soon. He'd docked his boat downtown on the water, not too far from the school. It had worked out easy as cake, took him less than ten minutes to get from the school back to Bedlam where he could gorge on horrific activities until visual overload. The night couldn't have gone any better, he was just sad it was coming to a close.

After all the semen had left his vessel, Hershel had a strange sort of sentimental feeling descend on him. After taking in the beauty of all the murder, he was realizing something—Edmon had done so much for him. After the school massacre, Hershel had no further plans that involved him. That was where it was all supposed to end.

But now there was a feeling starting to whisper to him inside of his head. He realized what the voice was saying. He owed Edmon. Edmon had given him a joyous snuff film that would continue to satisfy him for the ages. It could be played on a loop, for all eternity, immersing him in a mindless self-indulgence.

Not to mention the different sickening stops he'd witnessed in person. The restaurant was heavenly, and the cornfield as well as the house call were just as memorable. The zoo was also quite a bonus since Hershel enjoyed seeing young folks get killed by animals. Every split second that they'd clocked together that awful evening held a powerful pleasure.

It was special, not in some cheap Christmas gift from a neighbor kind of way. It was special by the definition of the word itself. Initially, he'd just planned to leave him there to be killed by police or whatever the outcome was destined to be. But now, a voice was telling him that wasn't right anymore.

What could he do though? What exactly would a violent, depraved imbecile like Edmon appreciate or enjoy? Did he even have the ability to "enjoy" period? If so, was there anything that could trigger it? Hershel shifted his position on the bed when he felt something crumple in his pocket. He removed the contents to reveal the blood and shit spattered picture of Edmon's mother. Through the crusty dried feces Hershel saw an expression absolute kindness, one that he knew was profoundly missed.

YIN OR YANG?

The floors looked like they were painted a different color, littered with the wounded corpses and body parts. A pile of bone, gore, limbs, and skin was heaped in the center. It looked like a warzone, except they were all trapped in the same foxhole. The distressed cries of the few mangled and soon to be dead echoed through the tall room.

It was just a matter of time until everyone got their turn. To Edmon, he was just getting started. He finished stripping the meat of the pelvic region he'd grasped onto and set it into the tower of death before him. It was never enough. It would never be enough.

He walked away from the hot-blooded heap and picked up a few of the many lit pumpkins in the gym. He began to arrange each one individually around the pile of screeching carcasses. When he'd finally finished, there was a massive circle of jack-o'-lanterns that encapsulated the countless bodies.

Edmon turned away from the bloodbath he'd orchestrated, hungry for more. It was time to move onward, life was no longer an overflowing commodity in the gym. He looked at the girls' locker room door handle and then at the boys'. Edmon didn't have a preference. He didn't even know what a preference was.

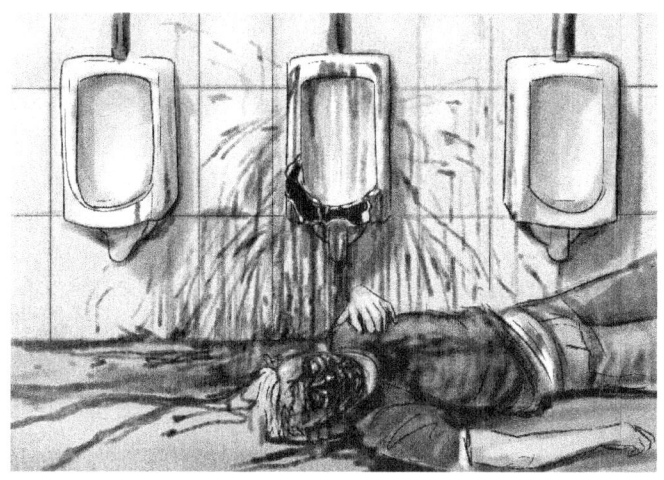

HIT THE SHOWERS

Jesse, Noah, and Charles checked both the exit in the rear and the entry back into the school. Neither was budging. They were all sealed shut so tight that a stout shoulder from Charles didn't budge it an inch.

"Great fucking idea, guys, now we're sitting ducks down here," Noah droned nervously.

"What are we gonna do now?" Jesse cried.

"I don't know if there's much we can do, except pray to God that he doesn't come down here." As the words left Charles's mouth, they heard the door break upstairs. It sounded more like an explosion than a door opening.

"Shit! That's him, we gotta hide," Jesse whimpered. They all ran for the bathroom instinctively. It was hard to make out everything around them, so Charles pulled out his phone. It couldn't call for help, but maybe they could use the light source to find a good hiding place.

The bathroom stalls seemed to be the only logical place to hide. They were also the nearest area available amid their rash reaction to heavy footsteps making their way down the stairs. When they opened the first stall door, a synchronized gasp emerged between the entire trio. Principal Richards sat dead on the toilet; his face looked horrifying in the darkness. It was distorted with the utmost suffering. They didn't have much time to think about anything else but opening the next stall. They started to hear Edmon's disgusting breathing echoing down the hallway, he was getting closer and closer with each chilling breath.

There were only three stalls, so Noah and Jesse took the one to the left of their deceased administrator and Charles took the one to the right. They all stood on the toilet seats and locked their doors behind them. The only thing they could do was be quiet, knowing the closed doors were only visually beneficial. They would do little to stop him if he truly wanted to gain entry.

Hunched silently, they just listened. The sickening gasping getting closer and closer to them. It sounded like whatever was out there wasn't alive. If they were only so lucky…

The noise was practically on top of them now. The dreadful cycle continued past the stall Charles had chosen. It stopped in front of the space in between them, the one that Principal Richards' corpse sat in. Edmon finished opening the already cracked door until it exposed the gristly sight. He didn't think twice and grabbed the body. He tossed it hard into the sink, causing the principal's already hardened head to collide with and break off the porcelain. As the sink tore off of the wall, water began to spray out everywhere.

It was unclear if Edmon thought he was playing

possum or just wanted to desecrate the corpse. Either way, it showed there would be no mercy, even in death. Jesse was trying her best to suppress her anxiety, but her tremors had let a low volume, panicked pant escape. Edmon moved in front of their stall and paused for a moment. Noah set his glossy eyes upon Jesse with a look on his face that said, "Goodbye."

He quickly slapped the stall handle into an unlocked position and bulleted away from her right into Edmon's arms. "RUUUUUUUUNNN!" he yelled out, sacrificing himself.

Edmon grabbed him by his man-bun and drove his face into the bottom drain of the urinal. Jesse and Charles slipped out of their individual stalls while Edmon continued to unleash his rage. Then a second time, he drove his already busted mouth square into the urinal trench and broke the bottom clean off.

Noah's jaw had cracked so ruthlessly that it was permanently unhinged and left dangling agape with the tooth count closer to Junkie Jim's. As blood pooled up piss, and part of a waning urinal cake expelled from his destroyed pie hole. Edmon paused the chaos and observed his destruction intently. As an artist, he only served to create different interpretations of himself. Noah was dead, but that didn't matter.

It didn't stop Edmon from putting his face through the rest of the remaining piss dishes. When one considered Noah's path and choices that night, their collision was a tremendous irony, which neither of them really ever know the entirety of.

Charles and Jesse were listening to him being ruined while still wondering where they should go. They ran past the sealed back exit to the row of lockers that stood up on both sides of the hallway.

Edmon dragged Noah's flaccid pulpy body into the showers next. He couldn't move or stand any longer so he lifted him up and launched him into the tiled shower stall separators.

He smashed him again and again until the walls were left with big chunk holes that led into the behind crawl space. Noah's body looked like a piece of human trash that had been crumpled by the hand of God and strewn aside. Like a glaring mistake that had finally been corrected.

"Where are we gonna go? They're all locked, dammit!" Jesse yelled frantically, pulling at each of the lockers to no avail.

"Shhhh! We have to be quiet or we're both dead. Come here, this one's mine."

He moved far down the row to the left-hand side. His trembling hands were still able to execute the lock combination flawlessly. Luckily for them, the football players got bigger lockers for their equipment, otherwise, they'd have an odd man out. Charles grabbed a hold of as much equipment as he could and set it down further away from his locker in the hope of drawing less attention to them.

As Charles finished moving the last of his gear out of the blue locker, Jesse noticed a note fall onto the bench. It read "Die Nigger!" As Charles made his way back to their potential hiding place, he locked onto it. "I'm gonna get those mother fuckers one day…" he mumbled as rage infused with his adrenaline.

If it was any other situation, Jesse would have said something, but instead, she just picked it up quickly and brought it into the locker with her. The thrashing in the other room had finally stopped and they could hear the gargantuan footsteps closing in. The terrifying, unmistakable breathing pattern kept getting closer again. Charles raced back quietly and wedged himself inside with her awkwardly. The discomfort didn't mean anything, they were just happy to get the door closed.

Edmon paced himself, passing the useless rear exit before reaching the last row of lockers. He reached both of his arms out to each side of the aisle and pulled the locker doors off effortlessly. Skip, the janitor, fell forward out of one and landed on the floor in front of Edmon. His body was clearly void of the most remote life-force, but this was irrelevant to Edmon. He stepped on his skull anyway, and watched his hellish hoof rupture the cranium open all over the floor. He kicked the hollowed-out sphere of humanity to the side and continued forward.

Edmon moved on to the next two storage boxes and pulled their doors off just the same as the last. The anarchic noise once again getting closer to Charles and Jesse. Doom was not just a few minutes away. Jesse looked at Charles, guilt simmering on her face. There was something she needed to release. She farted. It wasn't loud but Charles was close enough to hear it and, more disturbingly, smell it.

"Seriously?" he asked, disgusted.

"I get gassy when I'm nervous. Charles, I know we never really hang out or anything, but I have to tell you something," she explained over the crazy sounds of destruction nearing them.

"Okay… you better hurry before he gets here," he said, happy she was offering something to take the horror out of his mind momentarily.

"I actually like the remake of Dawn of the Dead way, *way* better than the original. I know Tom Savini did the effects in the original, and he's still my favorite, but it's just one of the few times that the remake has outdone the original."

"Okay... I didn't even know there was an original, but cool. I think since we are having our last moment confessions here, I should tell you. Not that it matters anymore I guess, since her face got ripped off…" Charles started to tear up. "I was fucking Ms. Mello, and she was really, really good."

Jesse looked back at him with a wrinkled brow. "No one ever thinks this when it's a girl, but that's kind of like pedophilia, isn't it?" Her judgment was cut short by what sounded like some sort of steam hissing closer to the violence. It was loud and separate from Edmon's thrashing. Suddenly, they heard the back door opening, followed by a voice they didn't recognize.

Edmon turned around and Hershel stuck his hand out toward him. Held between his grubby fingers was a tattered and fluid-splattered photograph of Edmon's mother from his file at the asylum. It froze him dead in his tracks, just as it had when Hershel had led him out of the Ladd Institute.

"You wanna see your momma, Edmon? I can take you to see her, I can take you right now. You just follow me and you'll get to see her, I promise you that."

Charles and Jesse couldn't really understand the whispers or exactly what was being said from inside the locker but they were thankful that Edmon had ceased his destruction. A welcomed stoppage after making your death bed confessions and believing you're about to be ripped to pieces.

Edmon began to slowly trudge forward toward the photograph Hershel held, almost like he could only see her picture and nothing else. Hershel backed away slowly into the woods and out behind the school.

Edmon followed him with the obedience of a man possessed; completely pacified and captivated. He was overrun with a feeling of nostalgia, the sort that only his mother had ever been able to stir inside him. As he stepped into nature's darkness, he felt an uncanny warmth in the frigid October air.

REUNITED

Hershel kept a safe distance away while Edmon trailed behind him until they finally reached the graveyard. He continued on languidly, his mother's photo being the bleeding carrot and Edmon played the hellish horse. Thankfully, the cemetery could be reached through the woods behind the school, it would be better if they stayed off the streets for the time being. There was no telling who might have been alerted to the evening's wretchedness already.

They'd brought the reaper to countless souls that Halloween, yet what the authorities actually knew was still the biggest mystery. He tried to keep the trail as clean as possible in an effort to prolong the events. But current day, as far as any kind of public murder went anyway, that was a tall order.

Slowly, they inched toward a specific gravestone, one that had an empty 40oz bottle littered carelessly upon it, and was still moist with urine. Hershel set the grainy photograph down in front of Emily's dark marker. Edmon gawked at it dejectedly, seeming lost in his own mind.

Memories of the minuscule moments of happiness he had by her side flashed on and off. Recalls of the only person he'd ever felt at ease around flooded back. While there wasn't anyone to confirm he could grasp the cold truth that his mother was dead and rotting, there was something that appeared on the surface at least to resonate.

A small tear welled up in the corner of his eye and beaded its way down his cheek into his fleshy mouth. Edmon bent over and picked up the picture of his mother off of the ground. Suddenly, a hazy mist began to seep from the soil below their feet and obstruct their surroundings. Their sadistic venture felt like it was coming to a close and as they stood in the cemetery, the aura was beginning to border on supernatural.

Hershel had never seen anything cloud up an area so quickly. Even for a sick, twisted fuck such as he, it was creepy. Everything about the place suddenly felt different than any other graveyard he'd ever been to.

He wasn't sure if all the things he was noticing were in his head or not. He was never someone to believe in the afterlife, or ghosts in particular. If they did exist, there would have been a whole fucking swarm of them swirling around him making his life hell. Instead, he just played in Bedlam, uninterrupted.

Seeing the freak upset didn't make Hershel blue (he was a psychopath that was impossible), but he knew it should have, these were the times when normal folks were supposed to feel emotion. So, he did something that he'd never done before—he pretended.

That was the best he could do for a kind gesture. As silly as it was to him, he pretended to feel pity inside himself as he viewed the final snapshot he'd be left with; Edmon still clenching the photograph of his dead mother as he staggered off into the black forest and disappeared in the dense Halloween fog.

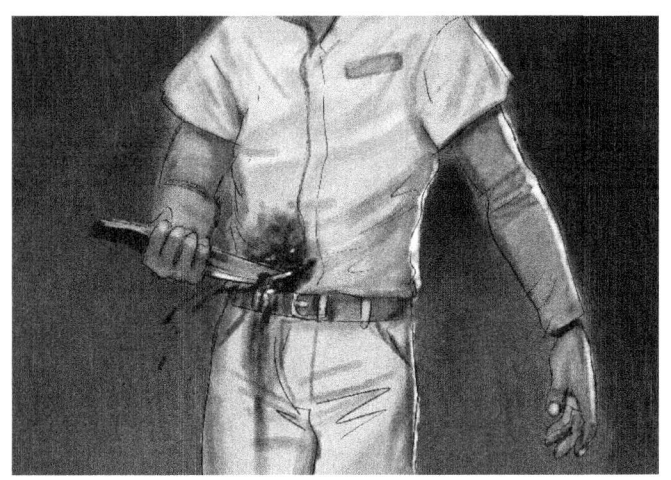

THE LONG
HALLOWEEN

When Hershel returned to the Ladd Institute, he readied his gut to harm himself. His wonderful evening didn't come without a price, as shown by the puddle of red he was laying in outside of what was normally Edmon's cell door. He knew the places to stab to avoid a fatal slice. Before the cutting began, he'd smashed his skull violently against the concrete for good measure. He'd returned a full two hours before the shift change, which was a hell of a lot earlier than he thought was going to be possible.

No one knew what happened inside except the final witness. The last man standing. His word would have to be good enough since all the cameras in the building had a mysterious malfunction that night. Hershel had seen to it that the way the malfunction occurred would be difficult to put their fingers on. One that would leave things open to speculation.

Surely it couldn't have been Lawrence, he was dead. Surely it couldn't have been Hershel, he was concussed and required thirty-one stitches and eight staples. What kind of psychopath would put themselves through that to help a lunatic escape? No one nearly loses their life over something like that…

Hershel dragged himself over to the phone, leaving a smear trail before dialing the police and explaining he was bleeding out. Lawrence would be to blame for Edmon's escape. Hershel had updated the schedules after their bet to reflect it was Lawrence, the new guy, who was scheduled to change him that day. The whole chain of events was rather unfortunate.

After the full investigation, the police would surely uncover that measuring the sedative dose inaccurately was Lawrence's fatal blunder. Just a simple rookie mistake is what they'd uncover. All of the evidence would be lined up tidily and available for the detectives. It would be easy to put together but not too easy. Hershel understood that if it felt too easy to them, they'd sense that something probably wasn't right. He arranged everything in a way that avoided that potential ensnaring misstep.

Hershel laid there in a pool of his own fluid feeling a little queasy. There were so many gruesome and arousing sights that fed into his fetish. Sick delicious sights that he was fortunate enough to observe over the winding course while following Edmon's odyssey. There was so much young gore and carnage to reflect on. It was all so very entertaining as he felt the warmth exiting his torso.

Yet as exhilarating as the gory details of the hellish evening were, for some reason, suddenly he couldn't focus on any of it. His brain screeched all the perverse memories to a hard stop, and as the puddle of red beneath him grew, the only thing Hershel could think about was who he should release next year.

ON A NOT SO
POSITIVE NOTE...

Trent sat slouching at the sticky bar of Larry's Lounge, his favorite dive. A cold Pabst Blue Ribbon was fixed to his hand and a mozzarella stick awaited his jaws—the final of the four. It was really convenient being that it was so close to his trailer. The Dolphin's game would be coming on any minute, but instead of Kenny Albert's face, he was seeing the large font running across the screen that read "BREAKING NEWS."

Trent looked at the bartender "What, did Trump get a new haircut?" They both laughed about what was considered "important" in the news cycle at the time. Then he saw the words "Rhode Island" pop up at the bottom of the screen.

"Rhode Island?" Trent whispered to himself, a little

puzzled. "Hey, do you mind turning that up for me, Larry?" he asked politely.

"Sure thing, boss," he replied, holding down the volume button on the clicker. "Hey, Rhode Island, isn't that where your ex lives? Your boy goes to school there, right?" Larry inquired.

"You, my friend, have a much better memory than me," he chuckled.

A news anchor began to spiel out the facts speedily: "In what is being regarded as the largest mass murder in New England, since the tragedy at Sandy Hook, we are heartbroken to report a body count that is being estimated, and we just want to be clear, right now this is only an estimate… a body count that is estimated at eighty-two. There's been unspeakable crimes, and a brutal assault on our youth. Authorities are still trying to determine exactly how many victims are associated with this sickening Halloween massacre."

"Holy shit, Larry! That's Winston's school!"

"Why, you don't think he's? You don't think…" Larry didn't want to put the idea out in the universe.

"Eighty-two fuckin' people dead, that's like a whole graduating class!"

The news anchor continued to provide details: "In what's now being referred to as the Bend Brook High Bloodbath, from what's been pieced together in the early hours, we know the following… last night, Edmon Black, a highly disturbed serial killer, escaped from his cell in the Ladd Institute, a facility for the mentally unstable. After murdering one orderly and leaving a second critically injured, he went on to take the lives of dozens of people. The killing spree stretched across multiple locations and culminated with the lock-in and slaughter of countless students at a school-run local Halloween-themed event."

Larry locked eyes with Trent for a moment apologetically and looked down, almost conceding his loss already. He lined up a free shot of bourbon for his likely foreshadowed troubles. They returned back to the report somberly.

"Edmon Black is said to have still been dressed in his inpatient wear. He's described as a white male, six-foot-seven, with an athletic build, and missing his… is this right?" The reporter asked a question to a man off-camera. "And he's missing his lower jaw…"

"We still have no idea exactly what's happened here but WPRI will keep you updated on the story. We have reporters on scene now that are going to give us some additional details. Let's head over to our live coverage where our correspondent, Dan Bell, is joined by some of the witnesses that were fortunate enough to survive this horrific ordeal."

Winston, Chaz, and Sara came into focus as a new feed established on the right side of the screen. The three were framed together, all looking like they'd been through the fucking ringer, but also relieved to be alive. Trent popped up out of his seat, confirming that the old expression "jump for joy" wasn't just that.

"That's my boy, I told you he wasn't no pussy, Lar!" They both hugged each other for a moment over the bar, something that didn't occur often in a bottom feeder shithole like Larry's Lounge…

The on-scene reporter approached Sara first, asking her to tell the audience whatever she could about what happened, then hanging the mic just below her trembling lips. A few pairs of flashing police, fire truck, and ambulance lights meshed together, creating their background.

"Almost everyone is dead… there was… there was so much blood inside. I'm not sure I'll ever be able to go back again." She broke down and began to cry, cycling through the images of her murdered friends that she caught a glimpse of on the way out. Both Winston and Chaz did their best to comfort her.

"I did a really stupid thing, I got really drunk and high before the dance started, and around the time when everything started, I passed out," Sara explained, still emotional in the process.

Sara looked over to the subtly smirking Chaz and Winston, her gratefulness amplified by her trauma. With each horror that she recalled, it left her even more thankful to be alive. The gory visuals of guts, limbs, pulverized humanity, and eminent danger boxed her in. In the moment, she felt claustrophobic.

It was dawning on her just how unlikely it was, the sort of miraculous feat that they had pulled off to save her when literally just about everyone else was dead. Sara looked back up at the camera, steadying herself, preparing to make a statement that she wanted the whole world to remember. She was finally able to control her emotions enough and continue speaking.

"I haven't been a good person. Truthfully, I've been a cruel, mean, and selfish person. But that all ends today. I just want to say that I'm sorry." She looked back toward the two boys that were responsible for her survival. "I always treated them like shit, but today, the reality is… I'd be dead if they hadn't pulled me out of there," she continued pointing back toward the school. "Winston and Chaz… are both heroes."

A NOTE FROM THE AUTHOR

I advise you not to read this note until you've read Scary Bastard in its entirety. I've had a few people ask me various questions about the ending of Scary Bastard, why I chose to let it play out like it does, and the history, as well as the future of this disgusting tale.

Why did you let the pair of sadistic, racist, rapists live? I understand that the point at which Scary Bastard stops might infuriate people, but there are a few reasons I chose this path. One being that sometimes the people that deserve to live don't always get to. In our real lives, many times it's the cut-throats and con-men that find their way to the top, building a legacy off of the doors they keep closed, off of what they hide from the rest of us. Such is the case with Winston and Chaz; they were ready to exterminate their peers until someone else just happened to do it first. A girl that they defiled was brainwashed by random circumstance into believing they were wonderful people in crunch time. In my opinion, the worst kind of evil isn't the evil you're aware of, it's the evil that is painted with so many layers, that by the time you get through to it, it's usually too late already.

Why didn't more people die? Well, I think PLENTY of people died, just maybe not the ones you were expecting. I think there are a few reasons for this in my mind. Many of the characters in this story (evil or otherwise), I truly enjoyed writing about, and I didn't feel like all of their stories could necessarily be told in a single novel. If you notice there are quite a few doors left open and I truly believe the stories don't stop there. Which is the reason I say above "the point at which Scary Bastard stops" instead of "when Scary

Bastard ends." I've made that a clear distinction because I'm in the process of writing Scary Bastard 2 right now! It's far from over and you won't believe where Edmon's story goes from here. I can't say when exactly this will be released but it should be prior to Halloween 2021.

As for the other characters, I see stories in their futures as well. Does Jesse ever go on to make the horror movie that she's been dreaming about since she was a child? Does Charles Buckley finally get his revenge on Winston and Chaz? Does the savvy child killer, Hershel Hughes, ever quench his thirst for bloodshed? Are the memories and videos of the Halloween he spent beside Edmon enough to satisfy him? My guess would be they aren't…

So, look for these stories and others independent of this saga to continue being released, and if you are interested in exploring the backstories of some of the characters or history mentioned in Scary Bastard, you can check on the following:

To hear more about how Edmon Black came to be, and the struggles of his mother, Emily, read the short story titled "The Donor" in my first book, "Try the New Candy."

To understand exactly what kind of a sick fuck Winston's father, Trent, is, read the short story titled "Did they Deserve it?" also in my first book, "Try the New Candy."

To explore the criminal exploits of the sinister alternative medicine company, Brinemax, which created the drug that saved Edmon's life and caused him to mutate, read my novella "Die Tommy."

If you wish to be added to my mailing list and learn about new releases, just email aronbeauregardhorror@gmail.com. Aspiring horror writers seeking advice are welcome to shoot me an email and I will try to respond promptly. I aim to help anyone chasing their dreams.

If you enjoyed the book and feel so inclined to leave a review or rating, it is greatly appreciated and serves to help other people discover my work. I'd also just love to hear what you think!

ORIGINAL SCARY BASTARD
1ˢᵗ EDITION BONUS ART

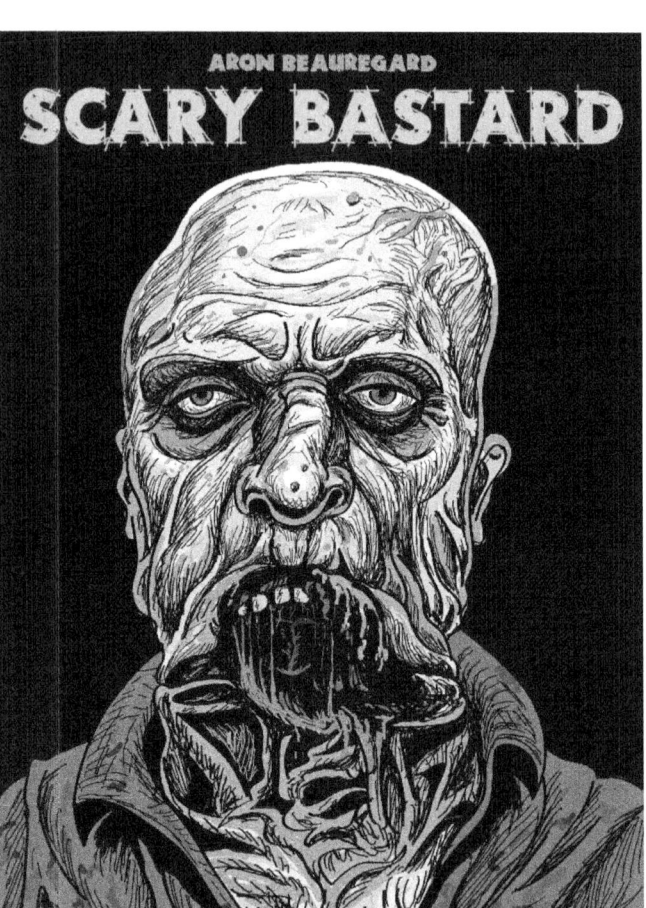

THE MADNESS IS MELTING BUT WILL NEVER DISAPPEAR

In the grips of a bad trip, the hellish and overwhelming delusions are inescapable. Scarier than the overpowering visuals and boundless paranoia is the promise that there's no way out. Are you prepared to take that psychedelic pilgrimage?

Are you ready to gaze upon an absurd growth that's gobbling up the entire world? Or take an unknown substance and hop on a private jet that spirals out of control? Would you let a young girl that spreads nasty rumors bend your ear to further her bizarre agenda? Are you willing to be paralyzed and stuffed into a coffin that's ejected into outer space, or overdose and have your consciousness transferred into a disturbed bird? These experiences merely scratch the surface of the lives you're set to live should you agree to take the trip...

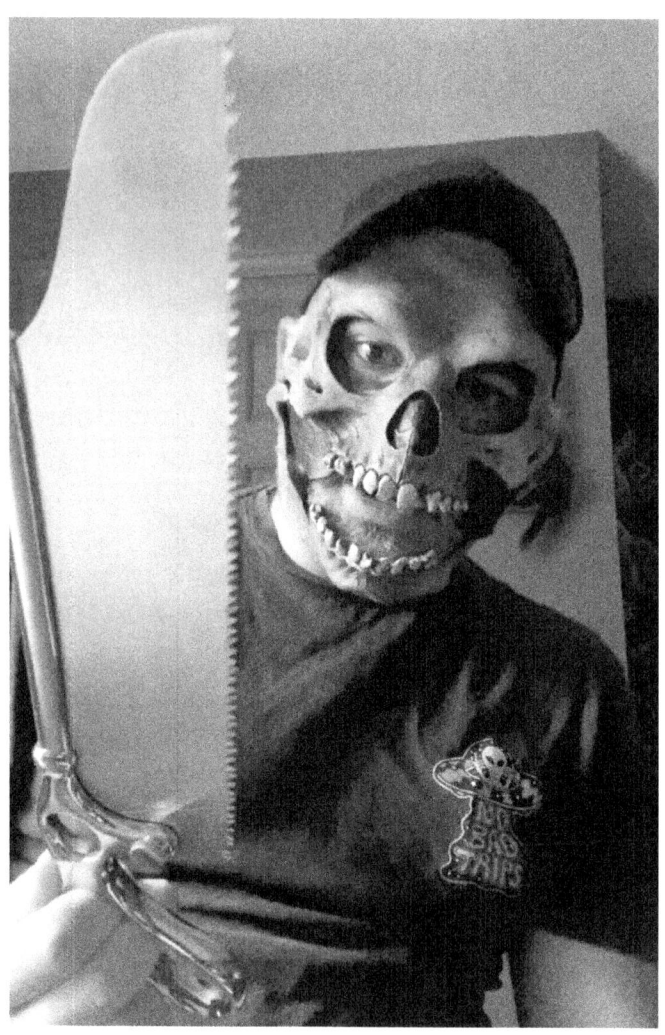

ABOUT THE AUTHOR

Aron loves Halloween. Ever since he was a young useless
bedwetter, when the macabre holiday was introduced to
him, he's been totally freakin' obsessed. His house looks
like Halloween all year. If you walked into his living room
on any given day, you'd be confronted by a seven-foot-tall
sinister clown and a plethora of realistic severed heads.
Since then he's also been infatuated with slasher films. The
two go together like candy and nuts, or knives and guts in
his eyes. Making an autumn slasher tale like Scary Bastard
has been a lifelong dream of his. And he finally made it...
and you finally read it… so now he can die peacefully…
but not before he releases Scary Bastard 2 & 3!

Printed in Great Britain
by Amazon

83252566R00129